The phone rang and Caroline jumped, her heart ricocheting in her chest. She reached for the receiver but couldn't quite bring herself to pick it up. Maybe she wasn't ready for this phone call after all. Karen would try again tomorrow.

"Hello." Caroline's voice was flat.

"Caro, T.J."

"McAllister!" She'd never been so glad to hear his voice. Or maybe she was just glad to hear any voice besides Karen's. She took a deep breath. "What's going on?"

"Zero. But I thought maybe we could catch a movie."

Tears sprang into Caroline's eyes at T.J.'s affectionate tone. He knew her so well; of course, he'd noticed how preoccupied she'd been lately. She wished things were easy and she was in the mood to have a good time. But they weren't and she wasn't.

"I can't go. I've got a test tomorrow," she told him.

T.J. signed off and Caro replaced the receiver gently. She didn't like lying to him, but she couldn't deal with him until she knew exactly what she was dealing with in herself.

The next time the phone rang, Caroline didn't hit the ceiling. She was calm now, and resigned.

It was Karen from the clinic. "Hi, Caroline. Well, you were right to come in and see us. The test was positive—you are indeed pregnant."

"Oh." Caroline wanted to laugh. *I am indeed pregnant.*

ON THE EDGE

Jesse Maguire

IVY BOOKS • NEW YORK

Ivy Books
Published by Ballantine Books

Produced by Butterfield Press Inc.
96 Morton Street
New York, New York 10014

Library of Congress Catalog Card Number: 90-93376

ISBN 0-8041-0447-6

Printed in Canada

First Edition: January 1991

To Sherwood Smith and Ellen Steiber—
thanks for the inspiration.

ONE

Caroline Buchanan sat on the edge of the rumpled bed and zipped her jeans, cautiously so as not to make any sound. Then she bent forward to pull on her black cowboy boots.

Flipping her long hair over one shoulder, she turned to look at the guy sleeping behind her. Craig lay with his face half-buried in a pillow, his brown hair sleep-spiky. *How come people look so young when they're asleep?* Caroline wondered idly. She took her watch from Craig's nightstand, checking the time as she fastened it onto her wrist. Lucky college boy—his first class wasn't until ten o'clock. Whereas Nowhere High opened for business exactly one hour from now. . . .

Caroline felt the mattress shift under her. Craig had rolled over. Now his hand fumbled at her waist and he tried to pull her back on the bed. "Where are you going? Man, it's still the middle of the night."

"The crack of dawn," she corrected, twisting out of his grasp.

Craig propped himself up on one elbow. "Stick around," he invited, yawning.

Caroline paused, her eyes resting briefly on his face. A nice enough guy, and very good-looking in a college-boy sort of way. The previous night had been reasonably satisfying. They met at a frat party the way they had the other two times they'd gotten together, spent a while drinking and dancing and shouting over the music, then headed back to his room. Some laughs, some pleasure . . . but feelings? Craig slumped back against the pillows. Caroline stood up, reaching for the jacket she'd tossed over his desk chair. No feelings.

"Can't." She didn't return to the bed. She wasn't going to offer a good-bye kiss, and she knew Craig didn't expect one. "Don't want me to get a tardy slip, do you?"

He chuckled, already dozing off again. "See ya," he mumbled.

"Yeah."

The battered steel-blue '65 Mustang was waiting at the curb in front of Craig's dorm. Caroline climbed in, immediately feeling more at home in her car than she had in Craig's bed. She smiled a tired smile to herself as she began driving away from the campus into the countryside. Sex was fine, but nothing set her free like getting out on the road in this old car.

She focused on the landscape flowing past. It was almost winter, she realized suddenly, and unusually cold. In the November dawn, everything was silver and snow-dusted: fields spiked with crop stubble, scattered skeleton silhouettes of lone trees, the crumbled brick of the abandoned factories that sketched a ghost town in the badlands north of downtown Redmond, Pennsylvania.

Caroline sighed. It didn't make much of an impression, this world. She'd seen the fields, the buildings, in every season and every light. There was no corner of Redmond she didn't know like the back of her own hand. But here she was, like always, driving around in circles. . . .

Not that it was anything new, the cruising or the staying out all night. One advantage of having just one parent, Caroline supposed; a divorced dad who didn't much care what she did with her time. The thought was flavored with only a thin taste of bitterness. It had been too long—seven years— since her mother ran out on them, and Caroline was too used to her dad's detached lifestyle and indifferent attitude to be much hurt by any of it anymore.

God, I must be getting old or something. She rubbed her eyes with the fingertips of her left hand. Used to be she could go without sleep, no problem. How come this morning she was so beat? Caroline squinted against the pale apricot glimmer of the sun's first rays, recalling the scene she'd just left. She sighed again. Not with regret—never with regret. The good thing about one- or two-night stands, nobody got hurt. An encounter with Craig was just a way to pass the time for them both. Her interest in him had never been deep, and at this point Caroline didn't imagine she'd see him again.

That fact didn't trouble her, but something did. T.J. McAllister. . . . *It's not like I'm cheating on*

T.J. by sleeping with Craig, Caroline reminded herself. She and T.J. weren't sleeping together, after all. And sleeping with Craig didn't mean anything—none of the guys she'd ever slept with meant anything.

For a while, though, she'd thought that old pattern was changing. Since she met T.J. a few months ago on the first day of senior year at Ernest Norwell High, Caroline had become a different person. Or she was in the process of becoming one; clearly she still wasn't there. *And maybe I'll never get all the way there.*

Abruptly, Caroline swerved off Route 58 onto Wilton Street to cut across town in the direction of her friend Alison Laurel's neighborhood. She and T.J. weren't getting there, anyway. It was really kind of ironic. It always struck Caroline that way, and she always had to laugh, even when the whole thing made her want to curse. From the first time they talked to each other, she and T.J. had been keeping each other slightly off balance. There was a deep connection between them—she was convinced he could read her mind—but only on a couple of occasions had that connection really brought them together, body and soul. Most of the time, there was an uncharted distance between them as they tried to figure out what it meant to be best friends—the first step, T.J. insisted, before becoming lovers.

Caroline had never tried it that way. She'd done without friends for a long time; she certainly didn't consider the guys she'd gone out with friends. Until T.J., she never realized what a complicated and frustrating and wonderful adventure understanding another person could be.

Frustrating's the key word, Caroline thought, slowing the Mustang to admire an old Victorian gingerbread house, fanciful and somehow alive-looking in the glow of the just-risen sun. She and T.J. had grown even closer since their crazy road trip to Philadelphia to rescue runaway Josh. Somehow, during that endless night, some of her carefully honed defenses had just slipped away. She never even felt them going. But now there was this Sandy person. . . .

Caroline coasted the Mustang through the stop sign onto Alison's road. Big houses with big yards gave way to small shoebox-style houses, and then to a row of spiritless apartment buildings. She braked in front of the building where Alison lived with her divorced mother and two younger brothers. She rang the bell. A few seconds later Alison appeared at the door, a box of cornflakes in her hand and a surprised look on her elfin face.

"Hey, Mouse!"

"Caro!" Alison's brown eyes crinkled in a smile.

"There's a donut and a cup of very black coffee with my name on it at the diner. Want to stop on the way to school?"

Alison looked at the cereal box she was holding and nodded. "You bet. Just let me grab my coat and books."

As they cruised in the direction of Main Street, Caroline started to feel brighter. With Alison for company, she almost didn't need the coffee. Mouse had a gift for warming people up.

Inside the diner, Caroline and Alison dropped

onto two vinyl-padded stools. Caro liked the no-nonsense waitress in the dingy pink uniform—she didn't even ask, just filled the coffee cups to the brim.

Alison bit into her donut, giving herself a powdered-sugar mustache. "This is the perfect breakfast, better than cornflakes. It's kind of like the morning, you know? With the early snow and all."

Caro smiled. Trust Mouse to make a crazy connection like that. "Coffee's my priority," she said. "The donut just gives me something to wash down."

"Well, I'm hungry today." Alison waved to the waitress. "Could I have a jelly donut, please?"

"Two donuts?" Caroline shook her head. "I don't know, Mouse. You could double your body weight eating like that."

"It's nerves," confessed Alison. "The first phase is pigging out, then later I won't be able to swallow a bite. Dress rehearsal is in a week!" Alison was singing the lead in *West Side Story*, the fall semester drama production at school. "You'll be there, won't you?"

"Where?"

"Opening night, silly. Dress rehearsal a week from now means opening night a few days after!"

Caroline grinned through the steam from her coffee. "Be there? I'll be the one in the front row clapping and whistling every time Maria opens her mouth."

"It will mean a lot," Alison said. "Knowing my friends are watching. Truly."

Friends. Not long ago, it would have been

friends and boyfriend, Caro thought ruefully. Alison's first serious romance, with super-jock Marc Calamano, had been intense but short-lived. That left friends. *Me, Josh, Darcy, T.J. . . .*

Caroline frowned. "Why the scowl?" asked Alison.

"Just wondering whether T.J.'ll be bringing a date to *West Side Story*," Caro answered dryly.

Alison got the reference, but she didn't pursue it. "Oh."

Sandy somebody—what's her name? A cute, preppy junior. *Can't be T.J.'s type*, Caroline thought, sipping her coffee. Then she smiled at herself. Like she had a right to say what T.J.'s type was or wasn't. Irony again. He'd just caught her off guard, taking a page out of her own book like that. What had ever made her think he wouldn't go out with someone else?

Caroline remembered the expression in T.J.'s penetrating green eyes when he brought up the subject of Sandy the other day. The two of them were hanging out at the deserted train station, wrapped in an old bedspread to keep warm. Sometimes Caroline and T.J. didn't need words—their eyes spoke for them. *I'm still waiting*, T.J.'s eyes had said. He was waiting for a sign from her, Caroline knew, and he was willing to wait because he loved her. They were both waiting for the time when they would be ready to change their lives for each other. T.J. didn't just want her body; he wanted her heart, her complete trust, and Caro had never given that to anybody. *Not yet, but soon*, her eyes had answered his. In the meantime, she still went out with other guys, kept her freedom. T.J.

with another girl, though; that got to her in a way she didn't much like.

Alison broke Caroline's reverie. "Homeroom in ten minutes."

They walked back to the car, Alison carrying a bag with one more donut for the road. "Thanks for picking me up," she said as the Mustang's engine roared to life. "This sure beat standing on the corner, waiting for the bus."

Pulling into the student parking lot five minutes later, the hot coffee glow had worn off. Caroline felt old again. Maybe it was just the season. The whole world seemed old and cold and dried up.

Or maybe it's because I've been in high school way too long, Caroline thought as she and Alison walked toward the sprawling brick building. She was ready to move on, had been for ages. The future was a blank, though. The stack of college applications on her desk at home didn't inspire her in the least, even though T.J. was trying to get her interested in the process, acting like he was her guidance counselor or something.

She'd always been psyched to graduate, to turn eighteen and get away from her dad and Redmond once and for all. She would finally drive in a straight line someplace—anyplace—instead of in the same old circles. Maybe not much of an ambition, but it was the only one she had. Now, however, it was starting to seem a little hollow. *That's T.J.'s fault too*, Caroline recognized. But college? She wasn't at all sure it was for her. Signing up for the Redmond City Scholarship contest had been a whim, a good excuse to wrangle with T.J., who was also competing. These days the novelty of rapping about books written a hundred or more years ago was wearing thin.

Leaving me . . . where? With a sharp rap of her boot heel, Caroline stepped onto the first of the concrete steps that led to the main entrance of Norwell High. *Here, for a while longer.* It was the only thing it seemed she knew for certain.

"A stick-up," John Hickham said, lifting his right hand with the fingers cocked, pistol-style. "Yesterday at Mayne's Hardware, right next door to Falkowitz's."

T.J. whistled. Josh worked a few afternoons a week at Falkowitz's art store, behind the counter. "Man, it could've been you! 'Your watercolors or your life.'"

"No kidding." Josh tilted back in his chair. "The cops came by after, asked if I'd seen anybody funny. You know, like maybe some guy with a stocking over his head might have been window-shopping or something."

The door to Mrs. Simison's homeroom banged open—enter another cluster of students. T.J. glanced over quickly.

Nope, no Caroline this time. Marc Calamano and Darcy Jenner made an entrance, though, gravitating to the back of the room where T.J. and Josh were encamped. Darcy looked tiny, T.J. noted, alongside the football star. Then again, the Incredible Hulk would have to crane his neck to look up at Marc.

"Hi, Darce. Hey, Calamano."

"Morning, Theodore." Darcy mussed T.J.'s hair

as she slipped into the seat next to his. Then she wrinkled her upturned nose. "Ever heard of this invention called a comb, McAllister? All the cavemen are using 'em these days."

He smoothed back his shaggy hair, grinning. "This is known as the rumpled look, Darce. It's supposed to be sexy. Drives the babes wild."

She tipped back her head and laughed. "Guess I must've missed your picture on the cover of the latest issue of *G.Q.*"

T.J. lowered his eyelids and looked superior. "It's not easy being on the cutting edge of fashion," he confided to Marc, now sitting behind him.

"You should think about joining a team," Marc responded dryly. He patted his well-worn varsity jacket. "Then you don't have to worry about individuality and stuff like that. You get your wardrobe and your hairstyle picked out for ya."

T.J. knew Marc wasn't necessarily a jock by nature; football just happened to be obligatory in the Calamano family. "Hmmm," he grunted, managing to infuse the syllable with a significant measure of understanding. Then he slapped a hand on his desk top. "You hear about Hickham's close encounter with the underworld kingpins?"

Marc looked interested. "Yeah?" He turned to Josh for the story.

T.J. sat back and let Josh do the talking. That was really all he was aiming for—just to get the guys talking to each other every now and then. Not that there was any actual animosity between them, but a little tension, sure, because of Alison. It had been plain while Marc and Mouse were dating that Josh was bugged. Now Alison and Josh were slowly starting something.

Women, T.J. thought, admiring Darcy's pretty profile as she checked her lip gloss in a compact mirror. *What they do to your life*.

Just as the late bell began to reverberate, the homeroom door bounced open one more time and two girls strolled in. T.J.'s heart stuttered to a momentary stop, then resumed galloping. Every time he saw her was like the first time.

Tall, slender, and curvy in cowboy boots and tight faded jeans, and a somewhat wrinkled man's shirt that came off as sexier and more feminine then satin and lace on any other girl. *No fair looking like that, Caroline Buchanan*, T.J. thought, a slow smile of welcome creasing his face as their eyes met. *No fair at all*.

He took his eyes off Caro for a moment in the interest of preventing his body temperature from hitting fever level. Plenty of other food for thought, anyhow. He watched Alison, dealing with her proximity to both Marc and Josh with typically beautiful delicacy. Marc was cool about it all, T.J. decided, mostly because he seemed to be secretly relieved. T.J. had gotten the feeling Marc wasn't ready to deal with the kind of serious relationship Alison had wanted. Meanwhile, Hickham couldn't keep the puppy love grin off his face. Did that bum out Darcy? A while back T.J. would have sworn she had a crush on Josh.

Josh, Darcy, Mouse, Marc . . . the friends he'd made since he moved to Redmond in September. They all mattered to T.J., but none of them like Caro. Nobody, nothing, mattered like Caro.

His eyes found her again as she came up the aisle toward him. He knew her so well by now that he could tell in a glance. The dark circles under her eyes; the way she moved, slower and without her usual lightness. *She didn't sleep much last night.* The realization was instantaneous. She didn't sleep much last night, and T.J. had a good idea of why.

His smile didn't change but inside T.J. was stabbed by a familiar, maybe unreasonable, but inevitable hurt. She felt like part of him, but she wasn't his. Not by a long shot.

TWO

"All I can say is, this better redeem us in ol' Macy's eyes," said T.J., referring to their strict and sour chemistry teacher.

Darcy grunted agreement as she washed out the last test tube. They'd just spent three hours on a special chemistry project; they both needed a decent grade if they didn't want to get warning slips for the class.

"I don't understand it." T.J. shook his head. "Always used to be a whiz kid at science. For some reason, I just can't get it together in this class."

"It's me," guessed Darcy. "I've always been a disaster in lab. My bad karma's rubbed off on you. Why'd you let yourself get stuck with me for a lab partner, anyway?"

"You were the cutest girl in the class," said T.J. Darcy threw a damp paper towel at him. "Hey, I was new in school. I was looking to get lucky any way I could."

"Yeah, right." Darcy stuffed her notebook into

her shoulder bag. T.J.'d gotten lucky all right. They'd both been on a roller coaster since they started at Nowhere High, him hot off the southern California beaches and her fresh from getting kicked out of boarding school. Not that she regretted breaking one too many rules at the exclusive boarding school she'd attended. Merton Hall was stifling, and she'd been eager to try public school. She just hadn't been prepared for how fast and furious the lessons in "real life" were going to come. She was still in the game, though.

"Where you off to now?" she asked T.J. "Need a ride somewhere?"

"Thanks, but no. My feet can get me where I'm going. The library," T.J. explained.

"But it's six o'clock!" exclaimed Darcy. "C'mon, let's go to the burger stand. I'm ravenous."

T.J. mustered his willpower with a visible effort. "I need to check out a bunch more books for the scholarship contest. A thick chocolate milkshake, though . . ." He licked his lips. "Nope. I gotta be strong. Feed my brain, *then* my stomach."

Darcy couldn't believe how seriously T.J. was taking the Redmond City Scholarship contest, but she gave him credit for it. "Well, so long. I'll think about you as I down one of those delectable shakes."

T.J. jogged down the corridor in the direction of the library. Darcy lingered for a moment outside the science lab. It was so quiet—she'd never seen the school one hundred percent empty like this. The overhead lighting seemed even more glaring than usual, with no life forms to diffuse its sterility. *Ugly,* Darcy thought as she wandered in the opposite direction from that taken by T.J. *Ugly as sin*. Preferable, though, to the slick ivy-covered beauty of Merton. Public school was no picnic, but at least here she could think the way she liked. She'd made some friends who weren't just Barbie and Ken doll clones of their parents and grandparents before them.

Darcy reached the big double doors to the auditorium. Rehearsal for the school musical *West Side Story* was in progress; Josh would be there working on the sets.

Darcy opened one of the doors and slipped inside. For a few minutes, she sat in a seat near the back of the auditorium, listening to the drama teacher, Mrs. Chin, dishing it out at Alison and a couple of the other kids. *Man, she's tough. Glad I'm a no-talent*. Then Darcy tiptoed down the side aisle, careful to keep in the shadows so as not to distract anybody.

Backstage was bedlam. Darcy couldn't imagine how the actors and dancers concentrated with all the hammering and yelling, not to mention the paint fumes. Still keeping out of the way, her eyes found Josh. He stood out from the other kids; he stood apart. Where they were all bickering and intense, his expression was peaceful. He was touching up one of the enormous flats, his paintbrush caressing the canvas like it was human skin. Darcy smiled wistfully.

They hadn't talked much lately, not since Josh ran away. Before that, although they went out together occasionally, it had become pretty clear that a romance by any normal definition of the word was not about to happen between them.

Somebody was playing the piano on stage, pretty badly Darcy thought. As a chorus of guys' voices boomed into song, Alison stepped through the curtain and crossed to Josh's side.

Darcy gauged their smiles as the two chatted for a moment. Even from a distance, Josh's glow was unmistakable. *I knew it from the start,* Darcy mused. It was natural that Josh and Alison should be attracted to each other, the whole Marc Calamano thing notwithstanding. They were both artists, both somehow not of this world. And it was equally natural that, no matter if they had fun together sometimes, Josh could never really go for someone like Darcy.

Let it slide, Darcy thought to herself now. What was the point? She didn't want to hold onto Josh; she had more pride than to push herself on a guy who wasn't interested.

But they were friends, and it had been a hard road getting there. It didn't have to be an exercise in humiliation, Darcy decided, just to let Josh know he didn't have to feel awkward around her.

Alison slipped back through the curtain, returning to rehearsal. Darcy stepped forward. Josh saw her and smiled. A nice, friendly smile; not the same smile he'd given Alison, though.

"These sets are gonna be sharp," said Darcy, admiring the two-dimensional New York City streetscapes surrounding her. Josh shrugged, but he looked pleased. She knew it hadn't been easy for him to get involved with the play and go public with his art. "Buy you a soda?" He raised his eyebrows at her offer and Darcy laughed, remembering the time she tried to take Josh out for dinner and the restaurant refused her charge card. "I swear, the soda machine takes my quarters."

Josh grinned. "Then okay."

They worked their way through the cans of paint and piles of scrap wood to the soda machine down the hall near the dressing rooms. Darcy fumbled in her shoulder bag for change.

Sweaty cold cans in hand, she and Josh sat down on a couple of metal folding chairs. Darcy watched Josh's throat as he drank half his soda in one gulp. "Thanks, Darce," he said after.

"Sure." She looked down at the can in her own hand. "Uh, Josh."

A wary look fogged Josh's clear blue eyes. *He probably thinks I'm going to be a total girl and give him one of those "Why don't you ever talk to me anymore? Don't you care for me?" routines.* "I, uh, hope *West Side Story* really goes well. Me and Caro and T.J. plan to see every performance."

"Great." Josh finished his soda, clearly primed to bolt back to his paintbrushes.

"Josh, I just . . ." *You don't have to make the Gettysburg Address. Just spit it out.* "I know—you and me—it didn't . . . But if you ever need a ride to school, or anything, just give me a call, okay?"

It was pretty feeble, but Josh seemed to get it. Slowly, his wariness melted into a smile. "Thanks, Darcy." They stood up. Josh slung an arm around her shoulders. Side by side, they headed back to the auditorium.

Wonder how many times I've ridden my bike over these ruts, Josh thought the next afternoon as he skidded off the dirt, shortcutting through the weeds for the last hundred yards to Split River Station. Ever since T.J. discovered the deserted railroad depot and shared the secret with him, Josh had grown addicted to its refuge. Well off the main highway on a dirt road to nowhere, the station was a perfect hideaway.

Today he didn't have time to hide out, though. His shift at Falkowitz's started in fifteen minutes— there was just time to grab the sketches he needed in order to finish his art homework that night.

At the door of the station, Josh hesitated, an uncomfortable sensation needling him. He didn't love the station so much since the time he found Alison and Calamano using it as an hourly-rates motel. Not that he was a prude or anything. He just didn't like to have to think about her and Marc that way. *Stupid*, he thought now, putting his hand on the door. *Makes a lot of sense to be mad at the station, for God's sake.*

Then he heard the low musical voice. The prickly feeling intensified and Josh froze. No. It couldn't be. It was over between those two.

Until he realized that the words he was hearing were lines from *West Side Story*, Josh didn't acknowledge how absolutely defeated he would have felt if it *had* been Marc and Alison in there, back together. Not that Alison had promised Josh anything, like, "you'll be my next boyfriend." It wasn't like that. Since she and Marc broke up, though, Josh had been hoping.

Now he stood quietly, listening. *She must really be starting to get nervous. Practicing out here all*

*by herself, when she's got a whole evening of
rehearsal at school still ahead of her.*

Alison's voice blossomed, rich and pleading.
Maria talking to Tony, Josh figured. His hand was
still lifted; he pushed open the door.

At the sight of Josh, Alison cut off her monologue
with a surprised squeak. "Oh!"

"Sorry," he said, wishing now that he'd turned
around and gotten back on his bicycle. He could've
done without the drawings. He was intruding.
What must Alison think, that he was there to offer
himself as her new leading man?

He spotted the sketch pad, lying on the green
sofa open to a Split River Station still life. "Just
wanted this," he explained, grabbing the pad and
stuffing it inside his jacket. "I'll get out of your
hair."

"It's all right," said Alison. "This is your space,
too. You don't need an excuse to be here." She
smiled. "And you're not in my hair."

"But I heard you, you know, practicing." Josh
was thinking about how he felt when he was
creating. It was a sensitive, private act; he hated
people watching, which was why it had been agony
at first, painting flats for the play.

Alison laughed. "The lines weren't written for
the empty air—they're meant to be shared. If I
don't have a real audience, I usually imagine one."

Josh had a goofy thought. *Maybe I'm in her
imaginary audience.* Then, *Yeah, right!*

"You're welcome to stay," she added, soft and
shy. "If you want to sit and sketch—if you don't
mind me. . . ."

Suddenly Josh realized he'd like nothing more.

To sit and sketch with Alison's warm, velvet voice wrapped around him . . . "I have to get to work."

"See you at rehearsal, then," she said.

A moment later, Josh was on the outside again. Now, though, as he listened to Alison speak he felt included in her expression. It touched him. He pedalled off, leaving Alison to recite the lines to herself, but with the feeling that there might be a part of him in her own private play. It would come with time.

"I'm flattered," Caroline said as T.J. dropped into the Mustang's passenger seat that night. "With the Wide, Wonderful World of Dating open to you, you called me."

T.J. shot her a grin. "What can I say. You're the only girl I know with a car."

Hitting the gas, Caroline laughed. "So you're just using me for my wheels. I suspected it all along. Where are we heading, anyway?"

T.J. slumped comfortably, his knees against the dashboard. "What do you think about bowling?"

"I don't think about bowling," Caro responded.

"Well, I've had my eye on Leftie's Lanes and Lounge for a while now," T.J. confessed. "In my quest to explore everything this town has to offer, I figure I should check it out."

"It's the place to go if you want to bump up against some of Redmond's finest," agreed Caroline. "But hey, I'm open. You want to bowl, let's bowl!"

"That's what I like about you," he said cheerfully. "You go along with my wacky impulses."

"You mean this wouldn't be Sandy's idea of a fun date?" Caroline asked. Then she frowned at herself. *Why the hell did I say that?* It was cheap; if she wanted to know about Sandy, she should just come out and admit it. She didn't usually mince words.

T.J. shrugged. "I don't know Sandy all that well. I can't say I know what her idea of a fun date is."

"But you plan to find out?"

"Sure. Why not?"

"Why not, indeed."

When T.J. didn't follow this up right away, Caroline glanced over and caught him studying her, his green eyes shadowed with an odd combination of sympathy and uncertainty.

"Do you want to talk about it?" he asked.

Caroline did want to talk about it, but she wasn't sure where to start. Her feelings were so mixed; she couldn't pin them down and name them.

She thought about Craig, and the other guys she'd spent time with since she fell in with T.J. "We can talk about it, but I bet we won't find anything new to say." Caroline swerved into the parking lot in front of Leftie's. "I'm a free agent and so are you."

"We don't have to play it that way," T.J. reminded her quietly.

Caroline killed the engine and set the parking brake. Then she twisted in her seat to look at T.J. "I know. Do you think I'm crazy?"

"Yes." He grinned. "Definitely crazy."

She put a hand out and ran her fingers through his hair, tugging at a strand. He yelped. "Take me seriously, McAllister. *I* think I'm crazy sometimes."

"You're not *crazy* crazy," he assured her. "But there's one thing you might keep in mind." His eyes slid away from hers. "You can love somebody, be in a relationship, and still be free."

Caroline's hand had dropped to T.J.'s shoulder. Now she lifted it again to touch his face briefly. "I'm working on that idea." Then she turned away, suddenly eager to be part of the noisy, neutral scene in Leftie's. "C'mon. Let's hit the lanes."

Inside, they tried on bowling shoes. "These things are disgusting," Caroline declared, displaying a foot encased in a tacky tri-colored leather shoe.

"You've got to wonder how many people's sweaty socks have been in there before yours," agreed T.J.

They walked over to the racks of bowling balls next and, as they did, Caroline noticed T.J.'s jeans. He'd rolled them up a few inches in order to look like a bowling geek. She punched his arm. "Lose the cuffs or you're bowling solo, buster."

"I just wanted to fit in," T.J. said innocently. "Remember, I'm still new around here."

Caroline went with the first bowling ball she touched. T.J. picked one up and pretended the weight of it was pulling him to the floor. Then he selected another and pretended his fingers were stuck in the holes. Caroline knew he was trying to make her laugh, so she tried not to, to no avail.

"Save it," she advised, laughing and hauling him to the only unoccupied lane.

They dropped their jackets on the bench and wrote their names on the score card. "How 'bout a bet," T.J. suggested as he swung his bowling arm in circles, loosening it up.

Caroline smiled. Here they went, facing off once again, as if competing for the Redmond City Scholarship wasn't enough. Was that what love was: a delicate duel? How much longer did she and T.J. have to go on circling, taking one another's measure?

"For what stakes?" she countered.

"If mine's the high score . . . you teach me how to drive."

"Teach you how to drive?" she echoed.

"Yeah, you know, as in 'drive a car.' I applied for a learner's permit today."

She laughed. "Clear the roads! All right. And if I win?"

"You name the prize."

She thought about that as they bowled, but T.J. started out with a strike and she never caught up with him. Which was okay. Caroline didn't think she was ready to win. Not quite yet.

THREE

Need air in the tires, Josh thought on Friday as he pumped his beat-up trail bike up the last hill toward his house on Briar Street. *Forget the air— need a whole new bike.*

Not even a remote possibility, of course; this set of wheels would probably have to last him until he was middle-aged. Sometimes Josh couldn't believe that someone his age had to worry so much about money. Most of the kids he went to school with seemed to do fine on allowances or part-time jobs How was it that *he* managed to luck into a step-mother who made him pay rent? *Rent!* And as near as he he could figure, you never stopped paying rent—that was life. Maybe throwing his money away on rent wouldn't hurt so much once he was working full-time at a real job. Since he quit flipping burgers at Jake's Place recently, and started working after school just at Falkowitz's Art Sup-plies, he made barely enough to keep his stepmother quiet and buy the occasional cafeteria lunch.

He crested the hill and sat back, lifting his hands from the handlebars. As he sailed down the other side, the cold November wind whipped his dark hair back and stung tears into his eyes. Josh punched a fist at the snow-threatening sky, then made a fast grab for the handlebars as the old bike started shaking. Small victories. That's what got a person by. He'd had one today at work, and it was sweet. He'd come up with an absolutely Nobel-prize brilliant idea, and the guts, to suggest to his boss, old man Falkowitz himself, that the store give him an employee discount on art supplies. That way, Josh had reasoned, he'd be able to buy even more paper and pens and stuff than otherwise. Falkowitz actually went for it! There were now half a dozen brand-new top quality drawing pens—fifteen percent off regular price—in Josh's jacket pocket to prove it. He couldn't wait to get to the desk in his bedroom and take them for a spin across a sheet of virgin paper. A new pen was better than a new bike any day, Josh thought. Who needed roads to rip along when they had an imagination?

In case he might be tempted to forget, his stepmother's station wagon in the driveway reminded Josh that the world wasn't perfect. Too much to hope for that he could ever just walk in the house and on up the stairs without being harassed by the Witch or the half-brats or, if he was in *real* luck, all three at once.

Bicycle dumped in the garage, Josh had to cut through the kitchen to reach the front hall and the staircase. And there she was at the kitchen table, his dad's young second wife, slapping her way through a stack of junk mail with her small mouth crimped in its habitual, put-upon frown.

"Like, I don't have enough work to do. Like I need another body to pick up after and cook for," she groused, to herself ostensibly but plenty loud enough for Josh to hear as he took two steps into the kitchen.

Another body? For a split second, Josh got a horror-movie chill up his spine. He pictured a baby, another spoiled blond half-sibling joining five-year-old Whitni and three-year-old Kyler.

Mrs. Hickham bitched on. "I guess I shouldn't be surprised. Why should I expect Jason to have any more consideration than his father or brother? Just to write out of the blue and announce he's spending two weeks here, over the holiday no less. As if nobody else's convenience matters in the least. . . ."

Jason! Josh braked, his sneakers squawking in protest against the bright-waxed linoleum. "Jason's coming home?" he practically shouted.

His stepmom raised her almost invisible, over-plucked eyebrows. Josh got ready for sarcasm, the usual stream of nastiness. She just tossed him the letter.

Josh fielded it and dropped into a chair at the table. He fumbled awkwardly at the flimsy airmail paper, his fingers still stiff from gripping his bike handlebars in the cold air. The paper ripped, but he got it unfolded. The cramped handwriting, unnaturally tiny and neat in order to fit all the news on one sheet . . . it looked urgent and exotic. It *looked* like a letter from somebody in the Navy, stationed in the Middle East.

Josh read eagerly, prepared to be disappointed. It occurred to him the Witch was making a cruel, unfunny joke. She knew what Jason meant to Josh, how much Josh missed his older brother. She was jealous of Jason, too, Josh had discovered, because she thought Mr. Hickham favored his older sons over her little monsters.

It wasn't a joke, though. "Hey, guys," the letter read. "Guess what?"

It's true, Josh realized, suddenly feeling dizzy and high. For the first time in a year Jason was coming back to Redmond, and not just for a couple days. This time he had a couple of *weeks* before he started his next assignment. Josh searched the letter for the date. His brother would be home by Thanksgiving.

He looked up, feeling a silly grin on his face, like he'd just fallen in love at first sight or something. He caught his stepmother staring, her pale blue eyes still tinted with irritation. For once, though, she didn't open her mouth.

Josh refolded the letter and placed it on top of the pile of mail. "Great news," he ventured boldly, getting to his feet and heading toward the door to the hall, shrugging out of his denim jacket as he went.

"Yeah," Mrs. Hickham snapped, rising also. She bent at the waist and started banging pots and pans around in one of the cupboards. "You don't have to cook and clean and grocery shop and . . ."

The list probably went on and on, but Josh didn't stick around to hear the rest of it. Hot air, anyway—he did as much mopping and vacuuming and stuff as the Witch any day. She'd always piled on the chores—hadn't even let up when she started making him pay rent.

Even so, things were different these days. The usually poisonous atmosphere was a little easier to breathe, Josh thought. He still got out of the house every chance he could, but the escape impulse wasn't quite as urgent as it used to be. Used to be his family—if you could call it that, people you didn't even *like*—his family made him feel wrong. Like he looked wrong, acted wrong, smelled wrong, *was* wrong. Ever since Jason graduated and joined the Navy two and a half years ago, Josh had been on his own. His dad didn't pay any attention to him, and his stepmom paid too much in a bad way.

Josh pounded up the stairs to the second floor, the bag of new pens from Falkowitz's clutched in his hand. He'd thought he was going to go through with it a couple weeks ago, after his dad's stroke. He meant to do it: run away and not come back to this house, these people, this town, Nowhere High—ever.

He turned his sketch pad to a clean sheet and arranged the new pens by color on the desk top, remembering how he'd felt then. Isolated, different, alone. Like a member of some kind of alien species that landed on the wrong planet. Unable to reach anybody, even his friends.

They'd reached him, though. He didn't run far enough or hard enough; he didn't get to the point where there was no turning back, although on the

unfamiliar nightmare streets of downtown Philadelphia he'd come close. T.J. and Caro had come after
him.

Josh selected a black pen. With a few deft,
distinct strokes he conjured T.J. up, right there on
the page. A cartoon T.J. with T.J.'s grin. Josh's
mouth twitched and he half-smiled back at his
creation.

"I owe you one, man," he told the face on the
sketch pad. Then he shook his head. No . . . that
wasn't right either. That wasn't really the way
friendship worked, Josh was finding out. You just
helped out when you could. You didn't incur debts,
you didn't pay *rent*. T.J. had come to his rescue,
just like Josh had come to the rescue for Darcy that
night at the station after she took a ride on the wild
side with Mr. Wrong. Friendship . . . it was like
a circle, a chain. Everybody was a link. He was
connected: that was what Josh had learned from it
all. T.J. wasn't about to let him take off into outer
space, never to be seen or heard from again. T.J.
had made Josh see he mattered in the Split River
Station scheme of things, if nowhere else. He
mattered to his friends, to T.J. and Darcy and Caro
and Alison.

Josh threw down the pen, the half-smile widen-
ing to a grin. For a few moments, he didn't
draw—he just enjoyed the pictures in his head.
Alison. He never thought about her in a two-
dimensional way—he saw her colors, smelled her
perfume, heard her music. The thought of her was
so full and rich he could almost put his arms around
it.

It was a lot due to Alison, Josh figured, that the
world seemed a little softer lately. Alison helped,

and since his stroke, Josh's dad was easing up at the bank and easing back into touch with the world outside the office. Even the Witch might not be sporting a halo, but she'd let some of her hard edges blur into an approximation of humanity. The nagging that used to be like nails hammered into his skull was pretty much just noise now. Every now and then she and Josh actually had a *conversation*.

And Jason was coming home. Josh seized the pen and sketched, this time a picture of his big brother. In uniform, tall and solid, a hero.

"Man, I can barely feel my fingers." T.J. tossed a dart and missed the bull's-eye by about a foot. "Gonna have to find ourselves a new hideout soon."

Josh blew on his hands and then took aim himself. His dart practically missed the board altogether. "For keeping warm, this isn't the pastime," he agreed.

T.J. sent the next dart off at random. It hit a black-and-white poster of James Dean right in the nose. "Sorry, dude," he said, carefully removing the dart. Then he crossed the room to the battery-operated space heater. Its grill glowed red, but the warmth didn't penetrate the thin, icy air for more than a yard or so.

T.J. spread his fingers over the heater and looked critically around the old railroad station. Nope, no way to further insulate the place. There was plastic over all the windows, and the door fit tight. Too tight—it required a wrestling match, sometimes, to get it open. Just no keeping out winter, it looked like. They'd have to live with it until the world thawed out again.

His hands warmed up, T.J. felt fond of the place again. *It's been good to us.* When he was first introduced to Split River Station in September by Alison's little brother, it provided shelter from the rain and the jackasses who'd dumped him from a speeding car by way of initiation to Redmond. Since then, they'd all made use of it. For Josh, it was a studio; one wall was in the process of becoming a mural, bigger and more dramatic than even the flats he'd painted for the play at school. They all did homework there, listened to music, partied. The green three-legged couch was piled with old bedspreads—T.J. himself had spent more than one night there, and he knew he wasn't the only one. For all of them it was a retreat, home base when home itself became unbearable. *Marc and Alison fell in love here. Fell in* and *out of love here. As for me and Caro. . . .*

He and Caro had swept and mopped and dusted until the run-down structure was habitable. They'd talked there for hours on end about every single subject in the world. They'd kissed there . . . and then talked some more. *The old chess game,* thought T.J. *Her move, my move. What do we want to mean to each other, be for each other? Love, sex, friendship: How does it all fit together?*

"Man, I almost forgot to tell you!"

Just in time, Josh's voice brought T. J. back to earth—his hands were too close to the heater and starting to get uncomfortably hot. He pulled them back and pushed them into his pockets. "Tell me what?"

"My brother, Jason." Josh side-armed a dart and hit the bull's-eye. "He's coming home for Thanksgiving, in between assignments."

Speaking of bull's-eyes, it would've been hard to miss his friend's enthusiasm. T.J. had heard a lot about Jason, who was advertised by Josh as the World's Best Big Brother. A sort of father figure, too, T.J. gathered. He had to be, with Mr. Hickham, as far as T.J. could tell at least, being basically a shadow figure.

"Mr. Navy, huh?" T.J. executed a back dive onto the sofa with his hands still in his pockets. "That's excellent. Good timing, too. You'll be done with the play by then, right?"

"Yeah. We got the letter yesterday, Friday," said Josh. "He'll be here a week before Thanksgiving and a week after. I pretty much can't believe it. Seems like about a decade since the last time I saw him."

T.J. tucked his chin into the collar of his jacket for warmth. "Too bad he can't stay for good. They sending him back to the Persian Gulf?"

"No—he got a domestic assignment this time. Almost as far off, though. San Diego."

"Sunny southern California." T.J.'s smile was wry. Talk about time warps. It seemed like a decade since he and his parents lived in L.A., but it was less than three months.

"Maybe I'll show him this place," Josh said thoughtfully. "Or . . . maybe not."

T.J. knew what was running through Josh's mind. Maybe not because maybe Split River Station would seem like kid stuff to a twenty-one-year-old naval lieutenant.

"It'll just be great to hang out with him," Josh went on. For a change, T.J. observed, Josh didn't need any conversational prompting. "I mean, just to talk and all. The phone connection to the Middle East isn't so hot."

"I bet."

Josh quit the darts and flopped onto the moulting bean bag chair next to the space heater. His bright blue eyes glittered. "He's the greatest guy," he said earnestly. "He's like . . . I don't know. He has his act together, you know? He's got it down. You have a good relationship with your parents—I've only got my brother. And ever since we were kids, he's stood up for me. I can always count on him to be on my side. He's always, kind of, with me."

With you? T.J. couldn't help feeling a twinge of skepticism. Yeah, the Persian Gulf was right down the street. There'd been nobody with Josh when T.J. and Caro picked him up in Philadelphia after a couple of days of living off the street. T.J. had gotten the feeling Josh had been basically alone in the world since his father remarried. "You make him sound sort of like that guy up there," T.J. commented, jerking his chin toward the wall where it was papered with pages from his favorite Superman comic books.

Josh narrowed his eyes; T.J. saw he'd struck a nerve. "I know you're not into the Navy thing," he said, defensive.

"Hey." T.J. lifted his hands. "I've got nothing against the man's career. We all make our own choices. Freedom, right?"

Josh shrugged, dropping his gaze. He kicked at an empty soda can somebody'd dropped on the floor, and it rolled, rattling, along the uneven wooden floorboards. "At least he knew what he wanted and he went for it," he mumbled. "He didn't waste any time—he got out of Redmond. Man, that's all *I* want to do."

T.J. exhaled a deep breath, pretending to focus on the white puff of vapor. He knew how Josh felt, but he was dubious about Josh's confidence that Jason, or the Navy, had all the answers. Josh idealized Jason, naturally. But you could take that sort of thing too far.

"Yeah, don't we all," T.J. said, staying neutral. Then he heard a car's engine outside the station. "And here's our ride out of town right now."

Mustang or BMW? he wondered as a car door slammed. *Caro or Darcy?*

Both. The door to the station grunted, then swung wide, letting in a sharp gust of November air and two gorgeous girls in sweatpants and sweatshirts.

"Couch potatoes!" Darcy called out cheerfully. "C'mon and get some food with us. Of course, *we've* earned it," she added, holding up her right arm and making a muscle. "Two tough sets of tennis."

"I'm in awe," T.J. said with his eyes on Caroline, whose smile of welcome was pretty weak compared to Darcy's. "But you're not the only jocks around here, you know. Me and Hickham just had two killer sets of darts. We're wiped."

Darcy giggled. "Tell me about it." Her glossy ponytail flipped over one shoulder as she bent forward to grasp Josh's hand and haul him to his feet.

"We thought Jake's Place," Caroline said. "Only if you can stand it, Hickham."

"Are you kidding?" Josh shook the hair out of his eyes, grinning. "I love the joint now that I'm not the one swimmin' in the grease behind the counter."

"Then let's go." She turned, and was out the door again before T.J. could reach her side.

The girls had arrived in the Mustang. T.J. dropped into his accustomed seat up front with Caroline. "Hi, there," he said as she turned the key in the ignition.

She glanced at him, her eyes big and tired. No trace of gold or green in the grey today. When she smiled, it was another feeble, half-mast sort of smile. "Sorry. Am I being totally spacey? Guess I'm just beat. Darcy had me running all over the goddamn court."

"Don't listen to her," Darcy advised from the back seat. "We each took a set. We both got a workout."

With a lurch, Caroline backed the Mustang in a half circle. Now the turn-of-the-century brick station, caught in a spiderweb of unused railroad tracks half-buried in earth and weeds, was out the right window. T.J. was watching Caroline, though, not the scenery as they bucked down the dirt road toward the highway.

Just a couple inches of vinyl-covered seat between them. He was conscious of her nearness, as always. Also conscious that for once *she* didn't seem to be conscious of *him*. She was staring straight ahead out the windshield like she'd never driven a car before. Except even though her eyes were glued to the road, she didn't seem to see it, either.

T.J. tried again for a response. "Hey, Caro. I got my learner's permit." Insurance rates had been so high in California he hadn't bothered trying for a license when he lived there. "I won the bet and you promised to give me some driver's ed. How's today for my first lesson?"

Not a blink. "Raincheck, McAllister, okay?"

"Sure. Raincheck."

At Jake's burger stand, T.J. hopped out of the car, reappearing a few minutes later with two greasy paper bags full of food. "Fries and cheese-burgers all around, I assume," he said, handing one of the bags back to Josh and Darcy.

Caroline was still facing forward, her hands on the steering wheel. At T.J.'s announcement, she sank back into her seat and dropped her hands. As if it took an effort, she turned to him, wrinkling her nose. "Not for me," she said.

"What, no appetite?" said T.J. in surprise. "After all that tennis, I thought you'd be finishing *my* burger, too."

Caro put a hand to her forehead and rubbed. She was pale. "Maybe some soda," she said, taking the cup from T.J. She stabbed a straw through the plastic lid. "I just don't feel like eating."

"Did you hear that, Caro?" asked Darcy with her mouth full of french fries.

"Hmmm?"

"Josh's brother Jason's coming back to town. You remember him, right? He was a senior at Norwell when you and Josh were freshmen."

Another "Hmmm"—Caroline couldn't have sounded less interested. And T.J. knew for a fact

that she'd had a huge crush on Jason Hickham in
days of yore when Jason was the big man on
campus.

She was sipping slowly, almost cautiously, at the
soda, like she wasn't sure if she was going to like the
taste of it. T.J. watched her, wishing for a minute
he could *be* her and know what she was thinking
about. Sometimes he felt so close to Caroline their
thoughts almost mingled. Other times, he might as
well be a complete stranger—it might as well be
the first day of senior year when she walked into
homeroom and didn't even give the new boy a
glance. This was one of those times.

And she had something on her mind, something
intense, T.J. could sense that much. By now he
knew, though, how Caroline operated. She'd tell
him about it when—and if—she was ready.

FOUR

A loose sheet of Superman wallpaper fluttered in a current of cold air. Lying on her back on the sagging green sofa, Caroline remembered when she taped the comics up there, on T.J.'s birthday a month or so ago. Split River Station hadn't seemed so hollow and cold back then.

She stared at the ceiling through the white clouds of her breath. *Should hit the road,* she thought dully. She'd be late for homeroom. But she didn't budge; just kept lying there, stiff and cold, with her hands pushed deep in the pockets of her jeans.

She couldn't face school this morning. She couldn't face her friends. She'd just skip. Her dad didn't care. He'd write her a note; he'd done it more than once in the past. Reaching this decision didn't make Caroline feel any lighter. Something was still holding her down. A weight like she'd never known before was pressing on her. It had a shape she couldn't get her hands around.

Caroline didn't see the peeling, damp-mottled ceiling of the station. She was seeing something else, a little glass vial containing yellow liquid that changed color after fifteen minutes. The home pregnancy test she'd bought yesterday at an out-of-town pharmacy because she couldn't bring herself to walk into Pulaski's Drug right there on Main Street.

Early that morning, in the bathroom of her father's apartment, Caroline had looked at the vial for a long minute—the longest minute in her life—to make sure. She'd studied the color of the liquid with the bathroom light on, and then with it off by the faint natural glow of the dawn. She didn't want to believe the evidence of her own eyes, but finally she had to. Both ways, the liquid looked as pink. Unmistakably pink.

She'd taken a couple of deep breaths, then flushed the contents of the vial down the toilet. She'd buried the vial in the wastebasket under about half a box of tissues, taken a shower, dressed, and made a break for the Mustang. As soon as she was strapped in behind the steering wheel, Caroline had hit the gas, trying to put as much distance as possible between herself and the realization. No matter how fast she drove, though, it kept up with her. It had followed her to Split River Station and was there with her now.

She'd started suspecting when her period was later and later. Typically with things she didn't want to think about, Caroline just ignored them. If you waited a problem out, it usually went away. This wasn't like that. She couldn't win by waiting it out.

Each passing day had only made the suspicion stronger.

I'm pregnant, she thought with disbelief. Then she said it out loud, her voice echoing in the empty station. "I'm pregnant."

For a second the words hung in the air, preserved in a white cloud. Caroline closed her eyes against them. Maybe the home pregnancy test goofed, she reasoned. Then she laughed bitterly. Supposedly those e.p.t. things were like 99.9 percent accurate; apparently a lot more reliable, anyway, than the condom she'd used a month ago with Craig.

Caroline passed a hand over her eyes, rubbing at the ache there. Craig. Thinking about him didn't stir any emotions in her, didn't add anything to what she was feeling or take anything away. Caroline knew Craig liked her well enough, but what they had was far from deep. She didn't really know him and he didn't really know her. She hadn't been planning to see him again, and she realized this didn't change that. *This is mine. Me. My problem.*

It was cold in the station. Caroline hadn't bothered turning on the space heater when she came in, because these days it only took the smallest edge off the chill. She couldn't have said when she started shivering, but now she discovered her whole body was shaking. She clenched her hands into fists and curled up her toes inside her boots, but nothing helped.

Then she laughed again. She could almost taste the irony. *Joke's on me. After all these years of taking precautions I finally got caught.* Funny, it had never occurred to her she'd end up on the wrong side of the birth control method safety-rate statistics.

She unclenched her fingers and gingerly placed a hand on her skin beneath her leather jacket and loose sweater. Under her hand, her stomach was flat and still and cool. A couple of days ago, she'd had some mild cramps and thought her period was on the way—that she was home free. The cramps had faded away, though, and Caroline's optimism along with them. Now her body didn't feel like anything in particular. She tried to picture cells multiplying like crazy. *How could something like that be happening inside me?*

Abruptly, Caroline sat up and jumped to her feet. Hurrying to the door of the station, she let herself out.

The sharp fresh air was an incredible relief. Caro gulped it in, hugging herself with both arms, holding herself together. It took a minute standing there outside the deserted railroad station, but gradually she began to feel braver. The complications began to creep into her brain—*What will people think? My dad . . . T.J.?*—and she dismissed them forcibly.

Slowly, her typical carelessness reasserted itself. Until she'd seen a doctor, she couldn't be totally sure. No point worrying about it yet. She climbed into her car and gunned the engine. The strong, familiar growl gave Caro's courage another boost. She checked the time on the dashboard. What the hell—she'd be late, but she might as well go to school anyway. She smiled wryly. It would keep her from *thinking*.

* * *

"It's just a workshop. Informal, you know," Darcy was explaining. "Actually, I've gone to a couple of these Career Office things and they're pretty good. I mean, obviously a lot of nerdologists will be there, but it could be helpful. I personally have no idea what to write my essay about." She giggled. "How about 'How I got kicked out of prep school.' Or, 'Cruising with Caro changed my life.'"

Darcy seemed to expect a laugh, so Caroline gave her one. Darcy kept looking at her, though, waiting for something else. Caroline shrugged, clueless. "What?"

Darcy lifted her eyebrows in a characteristic "Are you in outer space or what?" expression. "The college application essay workshop. Do you want to go or not?"

Caro was silent as she processed this question. Some dumb workshop on writing an essay for college applications? *Not for me. What would I write about, "How I got knocked up by Craig Stillinger?"* Caroline shook her head. "Don't know, Darce. I don't think . . . well, maybe."

"It's just a couple hours," Darcy said. "Everybody's going to have a partner, for critiquing each other's essays and all. That's why I thought we could do it together."

"So you don't get stuck with some total weenie geek."

Darcy grinned. "Exactly. But it's not just that," she added. "I really thought you might be interested. I mean, supposedly the essay's a pretty big part of what they look at on the application."

Caroline supplemented Darcy's reasoning. *And I need all the help I can get*. That's really what her friend was getting at in her tactful, roundabout way. What Darcy didn't know was that Caroline had pretty much decided not to fill out any college applications. But, of course, Darcy didn't know that. Darcy didn't know anything.

It made Caroline feel kind of odd as they sat there in the school cafeteria. This new, secret, almost-certain knowledge about herself made her different. Isolated, detached, from Darcy and from the whole Norwell High lunchtime scene. How would Darcy react if she came right out and dropped the bomb on her? Caroline could picture Darcy's face; it wouldn't be the first time she'd shocked her high-society friend.

Instead of answering Darcy, Caroline questioned her. "Since when are you so into this college application routine? I thought you were going to break the Jenner mold."

"I already broke it," Darcy reminded her. "I didn't apply early decision to Smith. And even if I get in, I'm not going there. But I have to go through the rest of the motions. I mean, what else would I do next year besides college?"

All of a sudden Caroline didn't want to talk about it or think about it. She crumpled an empty potato chip bag. Great lunch; lots of nutrition there. No sense pointing out to Darcy that she could work. As much as Darcy had lightened up since she started going to public school in September, she was still a little bit of an elitist.

"So, when's the workshop?" Caroline asked, resigned.

"Tomorrow after school," Darcy said in an exasperated way that made it clear she'd mentioned this fact a couple times already.

Tomorrow . . . Right before she met Darcy in the cafeteria, Caroline had ducked out to the smoking area behind the school, to the pay phone there. She'd made a call. Tomorrow after school she had an appointment at a women's clinic, for an official pregnancy test.

"I can't. Got something on the calendar already," Caroline answered, glad to have an excuse, even though it wasn't exactly the excuse she'd have chosen if she'd *had* a choice.

"Too bad. Maybe . . . Mouse!"

Alison had been at a meeting with her band. Now she presented herself at their table with a yogurt and two bottles of apple juice. Her tousled dark hair was held back by a bright Indian-print scarf and she was smiling. "Hey, guys. What's the topic?"

Caroline let Darcy do the talking. She was finding it harder and harder to just sit there, pretending to drink a can of diet soda and be a relatively normal Norwell High senior. Luckily she had a reputation for being reticent and private. No one was especially surprised when she kept quiet.

She watched her friends' faces as Darcy persuaded Mouse to be her partner at the workshop. They had nothing more serious on their minds than band practice and college applications. With a small twinge of surprise, Caroline realized she wasn't even close to wanting to confide in either of them. Not even close. And they were her best friends, next to T.J. It was almost sad.

The lonely feeling grew on her as she slumped down in her chair in the noisy, crowded cafeteria.

"So, I got my gas pedal, my clutch, my gearshift, my brakes."

"You got *my* gas pedal, clutch, gearshift, and brakes," Caroline corrected T.J. "And you better treat 'em right!"

T.J. chewed his fingernails, pretending to be intimidated.

She laughed. "It's really not that hard. Just takes a little coordination. Remember, you put the clutch in, then you shift. You've got to have the clutch in or be in neutral to start and stop. Right foot takes care of the gas and brakes, left foot stays by the clutch. Got it?"

They were in the Norwell High parking lot after hours, Caro having decided T.J. should take his first spin behind the wheel of her Mustang where he had the least chance of causing a twenty-car pileup.

T.J. closed his eyes. Caro laughed again. "Driving works better when you look where you're going, McAllister. Or are you praying for divine guidance?"

"I was just visualizing," he explained. "Clutch in, turn the key, clutch up, gas down. Okay, I'm ready."

Caroline gripped the passenger side arm rest. "Let's go!"

She had to bite her lip; the expression of concentration on T.J.'s face was comical. Veins stood out on the back of his hands, he was gripping the wheel so tightly. After starting the engine, he turned to Caroline, clearly pleased with his initial success. She gave him the thumbs up.

He popped the clutch. The Mustang lurched forward and stalled.

T.J.'s face fell.

"Bound to happen," Caroline assured him. "Everybody does that at first. Ease up on the clutch a little slower, and don't be shy with the gas."

This time, he made it into first gear without stalling. The Mustang started slowly forward. T.J.'s face broke into a slap-happy grin. "Hey, look at me. I'm driving!"

"Yeah, you're driving," Caro had to agree, smiling. "T.J. McAllister, King of the Road. Just don't forget to steer and stuff like that." They were nearing the end of the empty parking lot. T.J. showed no signs of changing course. "*Stop!*"

He hit the brake. They stalled again, a few yards short of the chicken-wire bounding the lot.

Caroline let out her breath in a rush. "McAllister, what do you think you're driving, the Batmobile? This car doesn't fly over fences!"

"Sorry," he said sheepishly. "Guess I got carried away with the intoxication of speed."

She shook her head. "Yeah, ten miles an hour does it for me every time."

"I'll try a circle this time."

"You do that."

It took T.J. three tries to reverse the Mustang, then they were moving forward again. He made a few laps of the parking lot.

"I think you're ready for second gear," Caroline observed.

T.J. depressed the clutch and shifted smoothly. "Hey, that was easy."

"Wasn't it? Yeah, it's the getting started part that's tough. And stop signs. Let's save those for next time, though."

"Tomorrow?" suggested T.J.

Caroline turned away from him to look out the window. Tomorrow . . . Just when she was having a good time. For a few minutes there, she almost forgot.

This time tomorrow she'd be getting the verdict at the clinic. "In a couple of days," she told T.J. "Shove out of there. I'm driving now."

T.J. looked heartbroken but obligingly climbed over the gearshift and into the passenger seat. He was quiet as she headed for his neighborhood, and Caroline tried to recover a lighter mood. "You've bitten the apple, McAllister. Now there'll be no stopping you."

T.J. agreed. "I'm already working it out in my head, how I can blackmail my folks into forking over the funds for a used auto."

"Bet you just want to learn how to drive so you can score with the opposite sex," she speculated.

She glanced at T.J. His amused expression told her that he knew what she was getting at, but she couldn't bait him into talking about Sandy this time. "It works for you," he joked instead.

When she didn't laugh as expected, T.J.'s green eyes clouded with contrition. "I didn't mean—"

Caroline shrugged. "Don't worry about it." *If he only knew* . . .

T.J. didn't ask her in when they reached his house. She knew he just assumed at this point that she'd pass on the invitation. He knew other people's homes gave Caro the creeps as much as her own did.

As Caroline pulled away from the curb, she watched T.J. in the rearview mirror. Walking up the driveway, his square shoulders looked thoughtful. If he only knew.

FIVE

Alison shifted the shopping bags from her right arm to her left, then pushed open the door to Falkowitz's Art Supplies.

"Sorry, ma'am," said a familiar voice. "We're closing."

She laughed, pretending to turn away to leave.

"Nope, nope, stop right there!" Josh practically vaulted over the counter. He reached Alison in a couple strides and stuck out his hands to hold the door shut. "What I *meant* to say is anybody comes into the store one minute before five-thirty gets a special bonus."

She smiled up at him. "What would that be?"

"The salesman's undivided attention."

"Don't know if I can handle it," she kidded.

"So, what's up?" Josh asked, moving aside to straighten up a paintbrush display.

"Just running some errands," Alison explained. "Trying to distract myself from the prospect of opening night tomorrow. I messed around at the

Salvation Army for a while, picked up a great old forties jacket and a beaded sweater. Then I bought some sheet music down the street at The High Note. Since I was in the neighborhood . . ."

"Well, hey. I'm glad you came by." Josh *looked* glad, Alison thought, gratified. There wasn't a trace of shyness in his manner today; he seemed full of himself, and full of life. "But I *am* closing the place up."

"That's okay. I'll help."

Josh bolted the front door and they wandered around the store checking that everything was relatively neat. "Didn't get around to dusting," he remarked. "Oh well. Gotta leave something for tomorrow."

They reached the rear of the store and flipped out the lights; Falkowitz's sank into a grey and quiet dusk. Josh ushered Alison out the back door and down the steps into the alley. His trail bike was there, chained to the stair railing. "Need a ride home?"

Alison glanced at the bike. "I took the bus here. I can get back the same way. Thanks, though."

"C'mon." Josh patted the seat of his bike. "It's built for two. It'll be fun."

She laughed. "Yeah? Where do you plan to put me?"

Josh considered. "The handlebars. How does that sound?"

"Dangerous!"

"It's not, though," Josh swore. "I've ridden with Woofer on the bars and I bet you don't weigh any more than him. Trust me."

Alison did trust him. "Okay. You're on."

Josh stuffed her packages into his backpack, which he strapped behind the seat. Then he straddled the bike and kept it steady while Alison settled herself as best she could on the handlebars. She started giggling as this went on, and when Josh pushed off, pedaling unsteadily at first, she laughed even harder. She closed her eyes as they wobbled out of the alley onto Main Street. "We're going to die."

"Trust me," Josh repeated, pedaling more smoothly now.

Alison opened her eyes. Looking down on either side of her she could see Josh's strong hands gripping the handlebars; looking up and forward she saw Redmond, the sunset gold and purple in the last rays of November light. A few minutes more and they were free of Main Street traffic and coasting downhill on a side road. "Hold on!" yelled Josh, his words caught in the windblown tangle of her hair.

Alison held on, feeling like she was on a roller coaster. The cold air stole her breath away. She couldn't say anything so she just relished it—terror, exhilaration, and over and around it all, trust in Josh.

At the bottom of the hill, the road levelled off and so did Alison's heart rate. Luckily the land was pretty flat the rest of the way to her neighborhood. She risked turning her head to look at Josh, who grinned at her. "Fun, huh?"

"Yeah," she had to admit. "No scarier than driving with Caroline sometimes, I suppose!"

Their momentum diminished and Josh had to work a little harder. Gingerly, Alison shifted her seat somewhat in order to turn her head more comfortably so they could talk. "You're a happy guy these days," she began.

A couple weeks ago, Alison wouldn't have made such a comment. First of all, because Josh was shy and didn't invite conversations of which he was the subject. Secondly, because he wasn't happy in the least.

With his dark hair whipped back from his sharply chiseled face, Josh's smile was especially pure and clear. "Yeah," he admitted. "I'm feeling pretty good."

"'Cause Jason's coming home?"

"That's one reason."

Alison turned her head slightly, letting her wind-scattered hair hide her shy, pleased smile.

They reached her block. Weaving slightly, Josh steered the bike up a driveway and onto the sidewalk in front of Alison's apartment building. As he slowed down, Alison hopped off the handlebars. "What a dismount," Josh cheered.

She laughed, stomping her feet to bring back some circulation. She liked flying, but it was kind of nice to be back on firm ground. "Come in for a while?"

She didn't have to insist. Chaining his bike to a half-grown tree near the stoop, he followed her inside. The T.V. was bellowing; her younger brothers Woofer and Benjie were watching. Her mom wasn't home, so she didn't have to start supper quite yet. Alison was glad. She and Josh could talk for a while.

"Hi, guys," said Josh as he and Alison passed

through the living room, stepping over Woofer and Benjie's limp bodies.

The kids didn't take their eyes from the tube, but their voices registered warmth. "Hi, J–Josh," from Benjie and "Hey, man," from Woofer. They reacted to Josh like his presence there was natural, Alison observed—Benjie barely even stuttered. Not like when Marc had come over and the kids had acted stiff or jumped ship altogether.

She led the way to her bedroom. With her brothers established in the living room, it was the only place to hang out other than the cluttered kitchen. She couldn't take Josh there; she had a distinct recollection that she'd left all the breakfast dishes sitting in the sink that morning.

She went right for the tape player, putting on some classical music. Meanwhile, Josh found something he liked—a sketch pad lying open on her desk. "Can I?" he asked, taking up the paper and a stubby pencil.

Alison settled on the bed, her back propped up by a stack of pillows. Josh sat on the floor, leaning against an old tapestry-draped armchair. "Sure. Go ahead."

"What were you working on here?" Josh flipped back a couple sheets of the drawing paper.

"Oh, costumes for the band." Alison wrinkled her nose ruefully. Her renderings of the band members weren't much better than stick figures. "Not much of an artist, am I?"

"These aren't bad at all," Josh praised. "You have a feel for line and movement." He looked up, his eyes glowing with sincerity. "Really."

"Well, they're just ideas," she said. "It'll be my

next project once *West Side Story* is over. The band is playing at the Christmas dance next month and we need a look. I'd like what we wear to be part of the whole *feeling*, you know?"

Josh nodded. Pencil in hand, he made a few quick marks on one of the figures. He held it up for her to see. "How about this? Is that what you were trying to get at?"

"That's it exactly!" Alison exclaimed, clapping her hands together.

Josh shrugged. "Just a suggestion." He flipped ahead to a blank sheet. "Keep working on it. You've got all the right instincts."

Alison tilted her head back, her eyes dreamy. That was it, really, instinct. The music she and the band created was made out of more than just sound. There was color, too, and shape—that's where the inspiration for the costumes was coming from. Music had a physical presence; when her band was at its best, their songs touched people, literally. Josh understood all this, Alison knew. Their mutual love of art in all its forms had been a first, true link in their friendship.

"Once I've got a handle on an idea for costumes, I'll have to do some more hunting at the Salvation Army," Alison went on, looking back at Josh. He met her eyes, and by the way his gaze stayed fixed on her while his hand kept moving, she could see he was sketching her. "Maybe you could come with me and help."

"Sure." Josh focused on the drawing now, his hand still moving without hesitation across the paper. Alison was struck by the picture Josh himself made. She found herself touched, and attracted.

And she wasn't nervous, feeling that way. Josh's
scrutiny didn't make her self-conscious. She was
perfectly relaxed and comfortable. It hit her then,
what a contrast it was. Compared to the times Marc
came over to her house. . . .

There was a book of poetry lying on the bed—
Emily Dickinson, one of Alison's favorites. She
lifted the book onto her lap and thoughtfully
thumbed the pages. She believed Marc had loved
her, in his way. But his way hadn't been her way.
Alison had learned from their experience that she
needed a different kind of love.

Like right now, she knew Josh wasn't sitting
there looking at her bed and thinking about sex,
which had been Marc's first response whenever
they found themselves alone. Josh liked her for
her—she knew that. But he liked all of her. He
looked at her with different eyes.

He made a last mark on the page. "Presto."
Turning the sketch pad around, he held it up for
her inspection. "My life-drawing class homework's
out of the way. Easy, huh?"

Alison faced the pencil image. The soft figure
curled on the bed, the profile against the curtain of
wavy dark hair . . . "That's me, all right," she
said with awe. But was she really that beautiful?
She blushed. Josh must think so.

"You're a great model," Josh remarked, casual
and appreciative. "Thanks for letting me use you for
my homework. I'd better be going, though."

And it was time for her to get to work in the
kitchen, Alison realized. "I'll walk you out to your
bike."

Night had fallen. Josh's bicycle was just outside

the circle of light from the doorway. Alison stepped out with him, hugging herself against the chill.

"See you around," she said, teeth chattering.

"You bet."

"The cast party after the show tomorrow night . . ." Alison began. She knew Josh still felt shy around a lot of the kids involved with the production. She also knew she really wanted to celebrate opening night with him. "Will you meet me there?"

In the dark, she could see Josh's eyes light up. "You bet," he said again.

He put a hand on the bike, then turned back to her, hesitating. Alison took the first step. Raising her hand, she touched his face lightly.

Josh held her gaze for a long, warm moment. Then he was off, the old bike rattling into the dark.

Sitting curled on the couch, Caroline drummed her fingers on the end table. "Ring already," she ordered the phone. She just wanted it to be over—she wanted to know the worst.

After the exam at the women's clinic, the nurse practitioner had told Caroline she was nearly certain Caroline was pregnant, but she would call her at home later with the official results of the pregnancy test. The nurse said she'd identify herself as Karen and not use the name of the clinic, in case someone else answered. Everything about the clinic was clean, discreet, caring, professional, and terrifying. Even to Caroline, who went in determined not to be rattled, who prided herself on always being in control. She couldn't close her eyes to reality at the clinic. She'd seen the other women and girls in the waiting area. Waiting their turn for exams, advice, abortions. . . .

Loud in the silence of the apartment, the phone rang. Caroline jumped, her heart ricocheting in her chest. She stuck out her hand and touched the receiver, but for a couple seconds, she couldn't bring herself to pick it up. Maybe she wasn't ready for this phone call after all. Maybe she should let it ring. Karen would try again tomorrow.

"Hello." Caroline's voice was flat.

"Caro, T.J."

"McAllister!" She'd never been so glad to hear T.J.'s voice, or maybe she was just thrilled to hear any voice besides Karen's. She sank back on the sofa, taking a deep breath to push her heart back into place. "What's going on?"

"Zero. But I though maybe we could do something. How about we blow off homework, hit an early movie?"

Tears sprang into Caroline's eyes at the sound of T.J.'s affectionate tone. He knew her so well; of course, he'd noticed how preoccupied she'd been lately. Here he was as usual, thinking about her and reaching out to her. She wished things were easy, and she was in the mood to have a good time. But they weren't and she wasn't. She was so edgy, she could never make it through a two-hour movie.

Caroline opened her mouth to speak then stopped, unsure what she wanted to say. She felt like one of those people with split personalities. Pretty soon she'd get that phone call from Karen—then she'd know which Caroline Buchanan was for real. In the meantime . . . "A movie? I can't. I have a French test tomorrow and I still have a ton of stuff to review." It was true, but she hadn't studied and didn't plan to. She'd take the F. "See you in homeroom, okay?"

T.J. signed off and Caroline replaced the receiver gently. She didn't like blowing him off, but it was the only conceivable move. She couldn't deal with T.J. until she knew what she was dealing with in herself. *And how will I deal with him, of all people, if . . .*

The next time the phone rang, Caroline didn't hit the ceiling. She was calm now, and resigned.

It was Karen from the clinic. "Hi, Caroline. Well, you were right to come in and see us. The test was positive—you are indeed pregnant."

"Oh." Caroline wanted to laugh. *I am indeed pregnant. Yes, indeed. C'mon, somebody, pop the cork on the champagne.* "Well . . ."

Karen knew just what to say. She'd probably made a thousand phone calls like this, Caroline figured. "You're only five or six weeks along, it's still early," Karen continued, her tone cheerful, soothing, practical. "You have time to give all the options plenty of consideration. It might help to come in again and talk informally with one of our counselors. Can I make an appointment for you?"

"Sure." Karen suggested a date and time. "Fine," Caroline said. "Thanks. Goodbye."

She hung up the phone and stayed on the couch, unmoving, her spine still rigid with tension. Karen's words repeated in her brain. *Talk informally with one of our counselors* . . . She'd go along with it—it couldn't hurt. Inside, though,

Caroline didn't believe in the concept of counseling. She'd always made her own decisions, figured out her own life, ever since she was a kid and her mom split, and her dad turned out to have zero interest in parenting.

There was more than one sort of counseling, though. There was the kind you could get at the clinic, and the kind you could get from a friend. T.J.'s image prodded her. Without thinking, she reached for the receiver. She could call him back, take him up on his offer, go to the movie, spill her guts. It would be such a relief. T.J. had the ability to comfort her like no one else could. T.J. was the one she always talked to.

Caroline stood up, turning her back on the telephone and the thought of T.J. *Yeah, right, tell him everything. Fun conversation that would be.* She put her hands to her eyes, pressing on them so that they wouldn't dare shed another tear. The fear washed over her and she had to recognize it for what it was. She was scared stiff. Scared this was going to be the one stunt that would drive T.J. away for good, forever. It was one thing seeing other guys. He understood her on that one, he could deal with it. But this . . .

She kept her eyes squeezed shut. She didn't want to imagine it—T.J.'s expression if she did confide in him. How could she even consider it, knowing how much it would hurt him?

The biggest problem of her life . . . her best friend. Just when she needed him most, he was the farthest out of reach.

SIX

Darcy gave her verdict at intermission. "Alison is a fantastic Maria. This is even better than the movie."

It was opening night of *West Side Story*. Caro, Darcy, T.J., and Josh had sixth-row seats in the Norwell High auditorium, which at the moment was a madhouse as everybody bounced around and yakked while they had five minutes in between acts. When T.J. ducked out for some air, Caroline had let him go without her. She had a feeling that if she ducked out, she wouldn't make it back in, and she had to stick it out until the end. It would be rotten to disappoint Mouse.

"She's magical," agreed Caroline.

"It's just so wild," continued Darcy, "the way she can totally transform herself. She's a different person up there on the stage."

Pretty neat trick, Caroline thought. She wouldn't mind being able to do that herself. Pick a character, any character. Only problem was, the play always

ended. You'd have to fall back into yourself sooner
or later.

T.J. collapsed into the next seat, his shoulder
brushing against hers. Caroline jumped.

"Didn't mean to scare you." He put an arm
around her and gave her a squeeze. "Why so
jumpy? The play getting to you? Afraid there's not
going to be a happy ending?"

Caroline bit her lip. If T.J. had any idea how
close she was to screaming, any idea how uncomfortable his nearness—usually so welcome and
natural—made her . . .

"I know there's not going to be a happy ending."
She flipped through the program so she didn't have
to meet his eyes. "I know how this story turns out."

"So pessimistic," T.J. chided. "Maybe they've
rewritten it. Maybe we'll be surprised."

"I'll believe it when I see it."

Caroline sensed T.J. considering her—considering whether to prod her a little further, try to
nudge her into a more open mood. To her relief, he
was distracted.

"Hey, kids. I see everybody's out for their annual
dose of culture."

Marc Calamano had hijacked a chair in the row
behind them and was resting his muscled arms on
the back of Darcy's seat. Darcy and T.J. both
turned to talk to him, but Caro kept her face
forward. At the best of times, Marc rubbed her the
wrong way. She didn't want to bicker with him
tonight; one push in the wrong direction and she
just might go over the edge.

"Caro."

She didn't have a choice. "Marc. What's up?"

"Found out we have a mutual friend—guy I knew at football camp a couple years ago. Ran into him on the strip last night—Craig Stillinger."

Caroline folded the program, pressing the crease hard with her fingers. "Hmmm."

"He played pretty good ball, if I remember right," said Marc, smiling.

There was no way she was up to joking around—about Craig, and in front of T.J. Caroline sidestepped Marc's marginally crude innuendo. "Yeah, he's on the college team, if I remember right."

The lights in the auditorium flickered. *Saved again,* Caro thought as Marc ditched to return to his own seat. The lights dimmed. Saved again, but not really. In the dark, she felt her eyes begin to sting with tears.

"I bet they rewrote it with a happy ending," T.J. whispered in her ear. "If I'm right, you owe me another driving lesson."

Caro nodded, not trusting herself to speak. She knew this was one bet T.J. wasn't going to win. There was no happy ending.

I did it! Alison exulted.

Until the curtain rose on the first scene of *West Side Story,* lifting the veil that separated actors from audience, she hadn't been certain she could really play her part. Sure, she could sing Maria, but could she *be* Maria? The countless hours of rehearsing, even the full-dress runs weren't proof. The packed auditorium was the test. Alison couldn't believe until *they* believed; at the same time, she'd known they would only believe if she believed first. And now the audience was on their feet.

Hands linked, the cast of *West Side Story* bowed to the cheers that filled the auditorium. When Michael Cohan, "Tony," pulled Alison forward, the ovation peaked.

Alison glimpsed her mother and Benjie and Woofer in the fourth row. The kids looked antsy, but Mrs. Laurel was glowing with pride. Two rows beyond that, someone was waving his arm like a windmill. T.J., winding up to toss a bunch of yellow roses onto the stage.

Laughing, Alison bent to retrieve them. She waved at her friends with the bouquet. Darcy blew her a kiss. But Caroline—hadn't she liked the show?—worried Alison. She was clapping, but mechanically. In the shifting spotlight, her distraction was apparent.

Alison didn't have time to wonder about it. The curtain fell and she was swept backstage.

Breathless and joyful, she let herself drown in the shower of praise. Arms reached out to hug her and she hugged back.

"Al, you were spectacular," declared Carrie Butler, the lead female dancer.

"Oh, you were, too!" cried Alison. "The dancers were all on fire tonight, but no one more than you."

Michael squeezed Alison's arm in passing. "Love you, Maria."

"Love you, Tony!"

Someone pressed a cold bottle of champagne into her hands. Alison set the bottle down, scanning the whirling sea of faces. She knew who she wanted to make a toast with.

Then the bodies parted and she saw him. Not Josh—Marc.

Alison froze. Marc walked in her direction, his broad shoulders somewhat stiff, holding one long-stemmed red rose. "Congratulations," he said in the deep voice that used to reach right inside her and melt her heart, a voice that could still make her flush.

"Thanks." As Alison took the rose, its sweet scent tickled her nose. She pretended to smell it, trying to hide her pink cheeks. "Did you enjoy the play?"

"Sure. You guys put on a great show. Who'd have thought it, seeing all the amateur night routines at try-outs."

She smiled. "We've come a long way since then."

"Well, you were the best one up there, but you were miles ahead of the rest of the bozos from the start."

Her eyes on Marc's face, Alison remembered auditioning for the play. Marc had watched, and she'd been singing just for him. Love had put beauty in her voice, but it was nothing, she knew, compared to the way she'd sung tonight. Tonight she'd sung for her family, her friends, Josh, the rest of the cast, the audience—but most of all for herself. It made all the difference in the world.

"I better split before somebody mistakes me for a dramarama," Marc joked. "See you around."

"See you around," she echoed.

Turning away, she tucked Marc's rose into T.J.'s bouquet. She knew where to look for Josh—on the fringes. He wasn't a center-stager like Marc.

She spotted him across the crowd. Their eyes

met and held; Alison invited him to her side with a
smile.

Josh didn't bring her flowers; he brought her a
soul as full as her own. "You did it!" he exclaimed.

"We did it," Alison said. And in the electric joy of
the moment, it was the only thing to do. She threw
her arms around his neck, and he caught her up and
whirled her in a giddy circle.

A moment later, Alison's feet were back on the
ground—sort of. Josh's hands still clasped her waist
and their lips met in a deep, sweet kiss. It was a
different kind of kiss than she'd ever shared with
Marc. It didn't make her feel like a stranger to
herself; it didn't pressure her and claim her. It set
her free.

When someone snatched the bottle of champagne from her side, Alison didn't protest. She and
Josh didn't need it.

"What's that?" Mrs. Hickham snapped suspiciously.

Josh had pulled a thick package wrapped in
white butcher paper out of a brown bag. He was
about to open the refrigerator door. "Steaks," he
mumbled.

Damn good steaks, too. He'd just spent half a
paycheck on them at Brickman's Fine Foods, the
best market in town. The Witch couldn't bitch
about grocery bills this way. Josh wasn't taking any
chances on her ruining Jason's homecoming with
complaints and boring casseroles.

"Steaks?" From the expression on her small-
featured face, you'd have thought Josh said worms.
"Well, there's absolutely no room in the fridge since

your father bought all that beer." She made beer
sound as distasteful as steaks.

Josh peered into the fridge, amazed. Since when
did his dad stock up on beer? *He must be as excited
as I am,* Josh realized. The man of stone, the
emotional recluse, was actually ready to celebrate
something.

"Steaks," Mrs. Hickham repeated, making a
point of elaborately sponging up a tiny spot of beef
juice that had dripped on her precious counter. "I
suppose a casserole isn't good enough for a naval
hero . . ."

Josh grinned. *You got that right,* he could have
said. But he didn't want to clash with her. He didn't
want to clash with anybody—he wanted the whole
world to be in harmony, for Jason. He wanted the
next two weeks to be perfect.

The timing couldn't have been better, anyway. It
was Wednesday, a little more than a week before
Thanksgiving, and *West Side Story* had wrapped up
the previous night. Josh smiled, remembering.
Another great cast party—he and Alison hadn't left
one another's side the entire time. Now except for
school and Falkowitz's, Josh's slate was clear. He'd
have tons of time to spend with his brother.

Mr. Hickham was in the living room, looking out
of place among the ruffled pseudo-Victorian lamp-
shades and doilies. The sports page was level with
his nose, a newsprint wall. He lowered it momentarily when Josh shuffled in to drop into a doily-
strewn armchair, then raised it again.

Josh actually felt disappointed, and he kicked
himself for it. So, his dad sprang for some beer—it
didn't necessarily follow that he'd been transformed

into the kind of father who was your best buddy. Josh had gotten a hair closer to the old man when he was laid up after his stroke, but of course the wall was still there. It was always there, with or without physical help from the newspaper.

Josh knew that Greyhound stopped in downtown Redmond. From there, Jason would catch a cab. And arrive home right about . . . now. A car door slammed in the driveway. Josh made it to the front hallway just as the door swung open.

"Yo, little bro!" Jason dropped his duffle bag and threw his arms around Josh in a bone-bruising hug. "Hey, Dad!"

All of a sudden, the whole household was crowded into the hall. Even the Witch and the half-brats, and for once Whitni and Kyler weren't torturing everybody's eardrums with their piercing whines. Instead, their mouths hung silently open as they gaped up at Jason.

He looked like something out of a movie, Josh thought. Tall, broad, his dark hair crisp and short, his blue eyes jumping out of his tanned face, and of course the final touch—the uniform.

"Son." Josh stared at his father now. He couldn't remember when he'd heard that much emotion in the old man's voice. Jason and his father shook hands, his father looking happier than he'd had since Jason left.

Then Jason nodded at the Witch. "How you doing, Audrey? You look great." He mussed up the half-brats' hair. Unbelievably, they didn't start bawling about it. "You all look great, guys. God, it's great to be home."

Audrey? Josh thought, his mouth still ajar. Calling their stepmother Audrey—Jason sounded so old. Josh never thought about her having a name; he didn't call her anything. "Audrey" actually smiled, too. Granted it wasn't much of a smile, but it wasn't her usual ice-queen grimace either.

Jason was looking at him again. He dropped his jaw, imitating Josh's gawk. "I can't believe it, Jughead. You got tall! I'm not gonna be able to beat on you anymore."

They grabbed each other, half-hugging and half-wrestling. Josh had grown some in the past year, but Jason still had a couple inches on him and quite a few pounds, not to mention muscles. Laughing, Josh tripped backwards and they stumbled into the living room, knocking into an end table. A couple of the Witch's tacky china figurines teetered and her smile crumpled into a shriek.

No damage was done, though, and Jason pinned him. He gripped Josh's biceps, testing them out. "You military material, boy?"

Josh grunted, trying to push his brother off him. "Give me a few months at boot camp, and I'll have *you* flat."

Jason released him, laughing. Josh sat up. He couldn't get the grin off his face; he still couldn't believe his brother was really there, in the flesh. Jason was back—his brother, his best friend. He wasn't alone anymore.

Josh socked Jason in the shoulder. "Nice uniform. Gotta get me one of those."

Jason scowled. "I can't wait to get out of it." He jumped to his feet, then hoisted the duffle bag and started upstairs, calling back, "Any beer in the house?"

Josh trotted to the kitchen. Mrs. Hickham frowned at him as he took a couple cold ones from the fridge. She was harping on the steaks again. "I hope you realize, Joshua, I'm not a short-order cook. You bought them—you can grill them."

Josh was in such a great mood, he wasn't even tempted to retort. Whistling, he sauntered out back to start the coals in the grill.

The steaks were a hit—Jason dug in enthusiastically, with Josh watching over every bite like a new mom feeding a baby.

"This is some chow," Jason said at last. "Don't get it like this on the carrier."

"You just make a list of what you'd like to eat while you're home," the Witch told him. "I'm going to the store tomorrow."

Josh came close to spitting out his food. Was he hallucinating? The Witch, who begrudged Josh every mouthful, was actually offering to grocery-shop especially for Jason?

"Thanks a lot, Audrey," said Jason, winking at Josh. "That's very generous of you."

Josh caught the wink, then observed his dad's reaction. Mr. Hickham smiled at his wife and she accepted the smile like a pat on the head. *Her reward,* Josh surmised. *She's just kissing up to the old man.* Domestic bliss; what a performance.

"Son." Mr. Hickham's voice was rough, as if he didn't use it any more than he had to. "Fill us in on the situation in the Middle East."

"If you read the papers, you know as much as I do," said Jason with a shrug. "These days it's business as usual in the Gulf. We're just keeping an eye on traffic and running drills. The real action is in Central America."

"Do you get bored?" wondered Josh. "Do you wish you were stationed in Central America?"

Jason pushed back his empty plate. "Not on your life. I'm ready for San Diego."

His brother left it at that, but Josh was eager to hear more. He'd hardly tasted his steak, and now he wanted dinner to be over so he and Jason could talk, just the two of them. He had so many questions. He wanted to know what the Navy was *really* like, and he wanted to tell Jason about his art class and the sets he'd worked on for *West Side Story*. He wanted to tell him about everything.

"You must be knocked out from all the travelling, son."

"Actually, I'm pretty pumped. The food helped." Jason tossed his napkin on the table and stood up. "Bumped into Steve at the bus stop—I'm meeting some of the guys at McSweeney's. Great meal, Audrey. Okay if I take the car, Dad?"

Josh swallowed his disappointment as Jason dumped his plate in the sink with a clatter, tossed his kid brother a mock salute, and split for the garage. Obviously Jason wanted to see his old high school buddies.

I'll get my chance, Josh reminded himself. Two whole weeks Jason would be home. That was plenty long enough to get to know each other again, to make up for lost time.

So much lost time.

It stung a bit. *Left with Dad and the Witch and the half-brats—again*, thought Josh as he rinsed dishes at the sink.

The minute Jason left the house, it was like he'd never even been there. The old smothering distemper settled back over all of them.

The Witch lit into Josh's dad. "I suppose Jason's going to take the car whenever he pleases, leaving me with no way to get around? Oh, that's just fine. . . ." Kyler squirted steak sauce on Whitni's baby-pink dress and she screamed like a banshee. Josh turned off the tap. Sticking his feet into his sneakers and grabbing his jacket, he ditched into the garage himself. Straddling his bike, he pushed off into the cold night to steer his way to Split River Station by the light of the hunter's moon.

Didn't think I'd be making this trip for a while, once Jason got home. . . . It only took a few minutes for Josh's fingers to feel thick and numb. He never remembered gloves. Didn't own any, come to think of it. What were the chances, he speculated as he approached the station, that anybody else would be hanging out on an icy night like this? Zero—no light coming through the cracks in the boarded-up windows.

As he used his shoulder to shove the door open, though, Josh heard the low sound of radio music. Caroline Buchanan was sitting on the couch in the dark. She looked up at him, her eyes wide and blank, like a wild animal caught in the headlights. Josh was just as startled—she was crying.

"Caro." Without thinking, he hurried to her side and put an arm around her shoulders. "What's the matter?"

"Oh." She pushed a tangled strand of hair back from her forehead. Not meeting his eyes, she laughed through her sniffles. "Oh, nothing, really.

It's just . . . it was a—a fight with my dad. That's all."

It sounded like a lie. Josh wasn't about to call her on it, however. Privacy. Instead he said, again without really thinking, "Where's T.J.?"

The question made sense to him. T.J. and Caro were best friends—they turned to each other, Josh knew. But the way Caroline reacted, you'd have thought Josh hit her. Her tears turned to fury. "What does T.J. have to do with anything?" she demanded, shaking off Josh's arm. "Does he have all the answers?"

Josh blinked as Caro stomped across the room, her boot heels punishing the wood floor. At the door, she turned back, giving him her profile. "Sorry about that," she mumbled, her eyes lowered. "I gotta split. See ya."

Josh hadn't seen the Mustang parked around back, but now he heard its engine roar. He was left alone with the radio, wondering what to make of Caroline's outburst, wondering what to make of the world.

SEVEN

Caroline flipped through the magazine. The glossy photos of brainless babes in Euro fashions didn't much interest her, but she had to put her eyes somewhere. Better the magazine than the kid in the chair on the other side of the waiting room.

Using her hair as a curtain, Caroline observed the girl surreptitiously. *Damn, she can't be more than thirteen.* That had to be her mother, sitting next to her and clutching her pocketbook like she thought she was expecting pickpockets instead of gynecologists.

She tossed the magazine down and looked at the clock. Three thirty-five on Thursday afternoon, five minutes past her appointment. Her gaze shifted to the bright Impressionist print on the wall. The sunny pastels were soft . . . soothing . . . false. Caro knew there were no blurred edges to the problems dealt with at the clinic. *The women who come here either have a baby or they don't. No maybes.*

"Caroline Buchanan?"

A young woman in white jeans and a pastel top had stepped into the waiting room.

"That's me." Caro got to her feet, acting relaxed, feeling like a death-row inmate called to the hot seat.

"I'm Maribeth." They shook hands. "Come on into my office."

Maribeth's office was more of the same—a Renoir, some Monet water lilies. And no impersonal desk separating judge and accused. They took the easy chairs in the corner by the window.

No case file either, Caroline saw. Maribeth must have read up on her in advance.

"Would you like a glass of water?" Maribeth put her hand on the pitcher standing on the coffee table.

A stiff shot of whiskey'd be more like it. "No. Thanks."

"So, Caroline," began Maribeth, her tone warm and casual. "I know it's only been a week since you learned the results of your pregnancy test. Have you been thinking over the situation?"

You've got to be kidding. Like I've had anything else on my mind. Caroline knew Maribeth meant the question differently, however. "You mean, have I been thinking about my . . . alternatives?"

Maribeth nodded. "The most important thing right now is for you to recognize that you do have options, a number of them. You may not have chosen to become pregnant, but that doesn't mean you don't have choices now. You aren't trapped."

"I *feel* trapped," Caroline said quietly.

"I know. That's completely natural. It's a lot to be

dealing with." She poured two glasses of water. Caroline took one. "Have you shared this with anyone? One of your parents? A boyfriend?"

Caroline pictured her dad, then Craig. Her father, then the father of her child. She laughed. "No, I haven't shared it. I plan to make up my own mind."

Maribeth nodded, taking mental notes, Caro imagined, to add to the file later. "Well, I'll be glad to help in any way I can. The women I counsel choose one of three options. Some of them have the baby. Some have the baby and put it up for adoption. Others choose an abortion. Each woman's circumstances are unique; each woman reaches a decision in her own way, for her own reasons. Are you leaning in any particular direction?"

Caroline shrugged. Wasn't it obvious? "I'm seventeen," she told Maribeth, her voice cool and steady. "I'm still in high school. I'm not married. I don't even have a relationship with the father of this baby. Wouldn't anybody else in my position have an abortion?"

"Not necessarily," said Maribeth. "It's true many would, but not all. Remember, you're not trapped. You shouldn't feel like abortion is the only way out."

For some reason she didn't understand, Caroline suddenly felt like crying. She ducked her head to sip at her water and buy herself a minute.

Maribeth turned to the window, ostensibly to adjust the miniblinds against the low afternoon sun. When she faced Caroline again, the latter had recovered her composure.

"It can be the best choice for an individual,"

Maribeth said gently, "but it's an idea most women find upsetting. I personally don't believe any woman should feel guilty about aborting an unwanted pregnancy, but there's often a sense of guilt and that has to be confronted. It helps to talk about it."

Caroline nodded. She'd talked enough for one day, though.

She placed her glass on the coffee table. "I've got to be going. Thanks."

Maribeth walked with her to the door. "Come in and see me again, Caroline. Or call any time. When you're ready to take the next step, whatever you decide, let us know."

The thirteen-year-old kid and her mother were no longer in the waiting room; a nervous college student type had taken their place.

Caroline hurried to the parking lot and the security of her car. She wasn't ready for the next step.

Help wanted, manicurist. Yeah, right. Caroline could imagine fussing over other people's nails when her own were usually chewed to the quick.

She strolled on at a leisurely pace, an idle eye on the store windows she passed. If the right help-wanted sign came along, she was ready to go inside and check it out. She'd been thinking over the idea of picking up a part-time job. It made sense to lay by a little extra cash, just in case . . .

"Caroline."

The familiar voice stopped her. She turned on her heel, her chin tucked in the upturned collar of her jacket and her eyes narrowed against the afternoon sun. "Hey, Craig."

He wasn't alone. She didn't recognize the girl. Just another cute sorority type, like the girl Caroline had passed on her way out of the clinic earlier that afternoon. They were holding hands.

"Haven't seen you in a while," Craig remarked, friendly and casual.

As they stood on the sidewalk facing each other, everything momentarily froze for Caroline. Time froze, and so did her heart. She hadn't seen Craig since she first started suspecting she was pregnant. Now the weirdness of the situation hit her head-on.

She was a real person, he was a real person, together they'd made another real person. But except for the physical part, they hadn't been close, and now for the life of her Caroline couldn't have conjured up one truly personal recollection of the time she'd spent with Craig. She didn't know what made him happy or sad; she didn't even know what he was studying at college. Emotionally, they were strangers.

"By the way, Caroline, this is Angie."

Caroline smiled at Angie. "So, what's up?"

Craig shrugged. "Not a lot. You oughta drop by the House some time. Like tonight—we're having a band and a bunch of kegs."

"I've got plans." Caroline heard the way her sense of detachment colored the words, adding to the message. *Don't call us, we'll call you.*

"Well, some other time." Craig put a hand on her shoulder, squeezing it through the cold thick leather of her jacket. "See you around."

"So long." She watched him and Angie cross the

street. Then she turned back to the help-wanted signs. She knew her instinct, to leave Craig out of it, had been right. Seeing him proved it. He didn't mean any more to her than any of her other random romantic partners, even now that she was carrying his baby. And she knew she'd just been a fling for him, too.

If she thought he cared even a little, maybe she'd feel like she owed him something. But they'd been lovers, not friends. He wouldn't be interested in holding her hand when she went to the clinic for an abortion, much less in raising the kid with her if she decided to have it. She didn't want his support. He had nothing to give her.

Caroline walked, her store window reflection keeping pace with her. A slim girl in slim jeans. A tiny waist . . . She tried to picture herself with a big basketball belly. All of a sudden she felt nauseous. She stepped into the doorway of the stationery store and leaned against the cement wall, her eyes pressed shut. Count to ten . . . deep breaths . . . it passed. She started walking again, this time back in the direction of her parked car.

She'd known for a week now—it seemed like a year. She'd thought the counseling session would settle things. She'd expected to come out of it and make one more appointment, this time for an abortion. Instead it had gotten her thinking in other ways. It had given her questions, not answers.

Should she have the baby, or not have it? If she had it, should she put it up for adoption or keep it? Caroline had no idea what she wanted. Most of the time, it still didn't seem real. She didn't look like she had a baby inside her, and most of the time she didn't feel like it either. Then there'd be a moment like that one just now—she'd feel sick, or get cramps. Plus she was tired all the goddamn time.

How can some tiny thing be taking over my life like this? It was like, against her will she'd been shoved over into the passenger seat. Somebody else was driving the car—her body.

Caroline unlocked the Mustang. Inside she just sat for a few minutes, her arms folded across the top of the steering wheel. She could still drive *this* car. But where to? She'd been avoiding Split River Station since the embarrassing encounter with Josh; she only spent time with her friends outside of school when she was feeling up and invulnerable. Couldn't risk anybody catching her with her guard down again—especially T.J.

There was a stack of library books on the passenger seat she'd been meaning to return—now was as good a time as any. Caroline stared at the books and thought about T.J., which she'd been doing a lot lately. Talk about a catch-22. Sometimes she felt so lonely and scared, she almost gave in and ran to him. She needed him so much. But didn't deserve him or his friendship anymore—not since this.

As she started the engine and drove in the direction of the high school, Caro thought, not for the first time, *Why couldn't it have been T.J.'s baby?*

T.J. crumpled a piece of scribbled-up notebook paper and tossed it into the wastebasket next to his library carrel. He couldn't concentrate on his *Walden* essay; it was going to suck.

He got up to sharpen his pencil, a classic pro-crastination move, just in time to catch Caroline entering the Norwell library with an armload of books. T.J. tucked the pencil behind his ear, know-ing the geek imitation would make her laugh, and approached the counter where she was dumping the books.

The smile she greeted him with was weak. She didn't even notice the pencil.

T.J. noticed something, however. The books she was returning were the books she'd checked out to read for the Redmond City Scholarship contest. "What's up? You done with those already?"

She shoved the books towards the librarian and then dusted her hands together. "Yep. I'm done with them."

"I can't believe you read them all. What a whiz kid."

"Oh, I didn't read them." Caroline crossed her arms. T.J. knew that gesture. It said: *You're not going to like this, but I'm ready for you.* "I'm dropping the contest."

Before he could control his expression, T.J. felt his face sag with surprise and disappointment. Caro's eyes narrowed, as if she could read his feelings and resented them. "Come here." He took her hand and hauled her back to his carrel. Sitting down, he pulled her onto his knee. She perched there stiffly, like a little kid who didn't have the least desire to tell Santa what she wanted for Christmas. "You dropped out?" he repeated, keep-ing his voice judgment-free. "How come?"

Caroline had one hand on the back of his chair. With the other hand, she took the pencil from behind T.J.'s ear and turned away from him somewhat to doodle on his notebook. "I decided the contest wasn't for me," she answered coolly. "Actually, I've decided *college* isn't for me."

"But, Caro—"

She dropped the pencil. "I was only doing the contest because you were," she snapped. "I was never in any danger of winning the stupid thing in the first place."

He digested this, sensing a hidden agenda. Something was wrong here. Something had been wrong for a while now. He slipped his arms around Caroline's waist. "What's bugging you?" he asked, blunt but kind.

Another surprise. Pushing T.J. back in the chair, Caroline scrambled off his lap like he'd bitten her. "Oh, just piss off, McAllister," she suggested.

T.J. thought he glimpsed tears before she bolted for the library exit.

One hundred percent baffled. In all the time he'd been around the mystery that was Caroline Buchanan, T.J. had never felt so far from understanding her. Wasn't it supposed to be the other way around? Weren't they supposed to be making ground, not losing it?

He stared at the doodles Caro'd made, a pattern of concentric circles. They looked like some kind of druidic symbols, and T.J. found himself wishing they meant something and could speak to him. He and Caro'd always shared a magic sort of private language made up of words, looks, touches. What happened to it? They hadn't been talking the same language a moment ago, that was for sure.

As he mulled over the previous scene, T.J.

82 Jesse Maguire

started to scare himself. Everything felt wrong
these days. Dating Sandy felt wrong, and getting
shut out by Caroline felt wrong. All at once, he had
a terrible thought. In all this commitment-shy
waiting around and getting to know each other
business, maybe he'd waited too long. Maybe
Caroline had gotten away from him.

EIGHT

Josh made up his mind as he biked home from Falkowitz's on Friday, blinking away dirt spit up from the tires of a passing truck. Jason—Split River Station. Tonight he'd take his brother there. Josh had been on the look-out for a time and place to rap; the station could do a lot of the talking for him. It was all there: his drawings, the mural, the fall-out of the last few, sometimes happy more often hellish, months.

I feel like I'm about to give birth or something, Josh thought as he jumped the curb to avoid the puddles icing up on the side of the road. For so long, the only outlet for his stories had been the sketching he did on the sly. Josh knew T.J. would always listen if Josh gave him the chance, and now he had Alison to share with. But there was a bunch of stuff inside him he could only give to his brother, the one person who'd known him forever.

At the house it was feeding time for Kyler and Whitni, and they must not have liked the menu because they were squawking like irritated chickens. Josh blew through the kitchen with his eyes and ears closed. He found his big brother in the T.V. room.

"Man, this can be a scary place," Jason observed. "Those kids are terrorists. They could hold their own in the Middle East."

"Tell me about it." Josh hooked a thumb towards the door. "So, you want to get out of here for a while? I know a great hide-out. Way out of range of the half-brats' noise."

"Sounds great, Jug, but I got help on the way." Jason's handsome face creased in a sly grin. "Remember Kim Foster?"

An old flame of Jason's. "Kim Foster Garcia, I thought."

"Yeah, well, I know for a fact she and her old man recently split up."

"I really don't get it," declared Josh. "You get hitched when you're like eighteen or nineteen, and then you're divorced a year later. That's not marriage. What's the point?"

Jason shrugged. "All I know is it works out just fine for me. She's still one beautiful lady, and she's looking for a guy to buy her a couple drinks, and I'm very happy to oblige."

Josh got it now. "Oh. So, you're going out?"

On cue, a car honked in the driveway.

"I believe that's the lady now." Jason socked Josh on the arm as he passed. "Don't wait up for me, Jughead."

Josh watched his brother comb his hair in the hall mirror. Then he was gone.

Amazing. The second Jason walked through the

door a few days ago, at least a thousand old buddies of his had crawled out of the woodwork. Jason slept in in the morning and went out at night. Basically, Josh hadn't seen him for more than five minutes so far.

Jason might as well still be in the Middle East, Josh thought, frustrated.

He dragged his feet in the direction of the kitchen, figuring to grab some portable chow and split for the station. If Jason wasn't sticking around for dinner, he'd just as soon skip the scene himself. Nothing for it but to try again tomorrow and see if he could get to Jason before another one of his old girlfriends did.

"The boys are meeting at McSweeney's, Jug," Jason said on Saturday. "Gotta be there."

Josh dropped his eyes, directing his disappointment at the rip in his sneaker.

Jason caught on. "Tell you what. Why don't you come along to the bar? Yeah, that's perfect. 'Cause you know, I wanna hang out with you, too, Jughead."

"The other guys won't mind?" Josh practically levitated with delight.

"Naw," said Jason. "You'll fit right in. Just don't advertise your tender age to the bartender."

They took their dad's car as soon as Mr. Hickham got home from work. Driving into town with the music cranked, Josh wished it could always be like this. Him and Jason—friends as well as brothers. Doing stuff together, taking on life together.

Nordecke Street was starting to stretch, a nocturnal beast opening its beer-light eyes after the day's sleep. Cold weather didn't seem to cut down the cruising, or discourage the girls from wearing their shortest, tightest skirts.

Josh wondered if his brother knew he'd never set foot in McSweeney's or any other of the joints on the strip. *I'm green,* he thought. Then he laughed at himself. Like the strip would ever be his habitat. He didn't see himself evolving into the kind of guy who pounded beer with his buddies every day after work. As for the girls, they looked great from a distance, but Josh had a hunch most of them wouldn't stand up to a closer inspection. Josh couldn't imagine Alison on that street, walking into one of those bars.

But tonight Josh loved the strip because it made his brother happy to be there. Jason gave an appreciative whistle. "What a sight, eh, Jug?"

"Yeah, it's a regular Fifth Avenue."

Jason laughed. "Might not look like much to you, Jughead, but you haven't spent the last year staring at other guys in uniforms just like yours with a regulation grey aircraft carrier and a ton of saltwater for a backdrop. After that, Redmond looks like a goddamn Hollywood movie set."

Josh followed his brother into McSweeney's, his hands pushed into the pockets of his jeans and his chin tucked in his collar, as if the less there was of him showing, the less likely he was to get carded.

They made it past the bouncer to the corner booth staked out by Jason's pals. Two beer pitchers were already half-empty.

"Yo, hey." Jason high-fived a couple of guys Josh hadn't laid eyes on since his brother's high school graduation. "Steve, Ben, Howie, Kurt, you guys remember my kid brother."

Josh slid into the booth, wishing Jason didn't have to say *kid* brother. Not that it made a difference. Steve and the rest weren't interested in him. Kurt pushed a foaming glass of beer in his direction, and that was the most attention anybody paid to him for the next hour or so.

Josh slumped back against the booth. His brother sat forward, elbows planted solidly on the table.

Howie and Steve had been grousing about their jobs at Rhiner's Mill. "Heard they cleaned up behind the scenes," said Jason, referring to the new corruption-free management at the mill. "That's gotta make a difference."

"Yeah, a difference of three hundred jobs," replied Steve, finishing his beer in one swallow. "They're talking lay-offs for Christmas. Happy holidays."

Jason shook his head. "Lay-offs. One of these days, they'll hit the Services, too. Can't count on the old Cold War to keep us warm anymore."

"I'd trade with you," said Howie. "I'd trade the mill for some time on the water."

"It's no love boat, man. Which reminds me, I've got a call to make. I guess Kim's house is feeling empty—she invited me for a nightcap."

The guys delivered the expected crude commentary. Jason grinned. Then he observed Josh's gawk. "Don't worry, Jughead. I'll take you home first."

Two more pitchers, more gab about sports, work, and women. Josh didn't open his mouth, and no one, including Jason, seemed to expect him to.

So much for brother-to-brother bonding. Josh

sipped his warm beer and went on waiting for Jason to come home.

Caroline backed the Mustang into a parallel parking space in front of her apartment building. Looking up, she found the living room window. It glowed yellow in the dusk.

Her dad was home, but his girlfriend's candy-pink Fiat was nowhere in sight. Funny, Caro thought. Usually by this hour on a Saturday those two were out bar-hopping, or else they were getting messy together at the apartment.

She crunched across some old grey snow to the sidewalk, jingling her keys. At the entrance to the building, she hesitated. Then she unlocked the door and crossed the lobby to the elevator. The Mustang would still be warm if she decided to retreat.

Mr. Buchanan was at the liquor cabinet with his hand on a bottle of Scotch when Caroline stepped into the living room. About to make his first drink, she guessed; his tie was still knotted. She knew from experience, though—an hour from now he'd look a lot less like a successful attorney and a lot more like a boozaholic.

"Hi," she grunted, already halfway to her bedroom.

"Join me, Caroline?"

Ordinarily she wouldn't even tap the brakes. The invitation was cold, an empty gesture. She and her dad lived separate lives; Caroline couldn't even remember the last time they actually had a conversation.

But tonight, for some crazy reason, she paused. *Who's doing this? It's not me,* Caro thought as she found herself pivoting on one booted heel to face him. "Sure. Got any club soda?"

"How about a shot of something in it," he suggested.

"No, thanks."

Major mistake, she realized as soon as they were seated on the couch, drinks in hand. She didn't have anything to say to this man, and he didn't have anything to say to her.

Mr. Buchanan sipped his drink wordlessly. Caro poked with one finger at the lime in her club soda.

"Mustang running okay?" he said at last.

She wanted to laugh. Of course he'd be more concerned about the old car than her; it would never occur to him *she* might not be running okay. "No problems there."

"Still seeing that McAllister kid?"

Her father was only interested in T.J. because of the lawsuit he was handling for Rhiner's Mill; Mr. McAllister was manager there. Once again, it didn't have anything to do with her. "Among others," she replied. Then she gulped down half her soda. Before she could bolt, though, the door to the apartment swung open.

Suzi breezed in, all perfume and fur coat and teased platinum blond hair. "Why, look at this," she squealed. "A little father-daughter togetherness. How perfectly precious!"

Father-daughter togetherness . . . Caro jumped to her feet, fighting back a sudden wave of nausea that was part morning sickness, part the usual gag reflex to Suzi's saccharinity. Meanwhile, Mr. Buchanan smiled. At Suzi; Caroline wasn't included in the beam.

Suzi climbed onto his lap and wrapped her arms around his neck. Caroline had no desire to witness the sloppy kiss that was sure to follow. Two was company . . . Her father and his girlfriend, who wasn't much older than his daughter, made a unit. Caro didn't fit into the picture.

And she'd fit even less when she had a big, unmarried, pregnant belly on her, Caroline thought as she dumped the ice from her glass in the kitchen sink. Her dad would probably throw her out on her ear.

She might as well live alone. For years, she'd had no mother, and for all purposes no father either. She'd never shared anything, would never share anything with him except maybe an aloof, chip-on-the-shoulder attitude springing from a common source.

Caroline started the shower running, then stripped off her clothes and stepped under the hot stream. Her eyes squeezed shut, she let the water run down her face along with the tears.

"Just you and Mouse, huh?"

On the other end of the line, Darcy confirmed. "Alison heard Josh was having a boy's night out with Jason, and that inspired us to go for a girls' night out. She's still celebrating her liberation from the *West Side Story* rehearsal grind. Are you up for a movie?"

Caroline twisted the phone cord around her finger, considering. Usually on a Saturday night she

could be found anywhere but home. Her father and
Suzi had gone out, though—they'd left by the time
she got out of the shower an hour earlier. For a very
pleasant change she had the apartment to herself.

The couch was awfully comfortable, and Caroline
was feeling basically antisocial. "Actually—no. Tell
you the truth, I'm not feeling all that well," she told
Darcy.

"Really? I'm sorry." Darcy sounded concerned.
"It *is* cold and flu season. Take care of yourself,
okay?"

Cold and flu season—Caroline wanted to laugh.
What would Darcy say if she let on what was *really*
wrong with her? "Yeah, I will," she promised.
"Have fun. Tell Mouse hi from me. Maybe I'll catch
up with you guys later in the weekend."

Stretching, she replaced the phone. Then on
second thought, she rolled halfway off the couch
and pulled the line out of the jack. *Off the hook—I
wish it was all as easy as unplugging the phone.*

She lay back on the couch on her side, a blanket
tucked up under her chin and her face to the T.V.
Using the remote control, she raised the volume
until it was cranking megaloud, just right for
drowning out thoughts. But her thoughts wouldn't
drown. Even the gun battles and sex and suspense
of the cable-channel movie couldn't distract Caroline.
She stared at the figures on the T.V. while she saw
different characters in her head. Herself, going back
to the clinic to have her pregnancy "terminated." That
was what they called it, terminated. It didn't sound
biological that way, or real; it sounded like something
you did to a malfunctioning appliance. Then Caroline
pictured herself a year from now, eighteen years old,

a high school drop-out in a low-rent apartment some-where with a baby. *I don't know much,* Caro thought. *I just know I don't want to be either of those people.* The whole thing was a nightmare.

Maybe she should've gone out. She could be with Darcy and Alison, or hanging out with Brad Gradowski and his buddies at one of their usual Saturday night beerfests. *Fun company I'd be.* She made herself laugh, thinking about it. *"Hey, Brad, what's with Caroline tonight?" "Aw, nothing. She's just pregnant."*

The T.V. was on so loud, Caroline didn't hear the doorbell the first time. Then it buzzed again. She lowered the volume, but didn't move. Probably some scuzzbag lawyer friends of her father's—they'd give up and split. Whoever it was pressed the bell a third time.

"Hold on," Caroline grumbled, tossing aside the blanket. "Keep your pants on, already."

Reaching the front door, she punched the inter-com to the lobby downstairs, ready to be her rudest. "Yeah, who is it?"

"It's me."

"Me?"

"T.J."

"T.J.!" It hadn't sounded like him through the intercom crackle. "Well . . . come on up." Car-oline pressed the button that unlocked the lobby entrance. Then she had two whole minutes while T.J. was waiting for the elevator to figure out how she was going to handle him.

Because it wasn't safe. T.J. knew her too damn well. She couldn't pretend her tantrum in the library a few days ago was a result of PMS. Not that he'd bring it up, but somehow the conversation would get around to being personal. With T.J. it always was. They never just talked about the weather; they couldn't be purely superficial and casual with each other.

Caroline heard the rap of knuckles on wood. She opened the door, and there was T.J., shifting his weight from foot to foot like he wasn't sure what kind of welcome he was going to get.

"If you're looking for a candy bar, you're out of luck," she said lightly, so he'd know right off the bat she wasn't still mad at him. "Halloween was *last* month."

T.J. got the hold-fire message. He pretended to be disappointed. "And I suppose I'm too early for pumpkin pie and turkey."

She laughed. "Way too early. We're not into that routine here. Our Thanksgiving tradition is that my dad takes his current babe out to a French restaurant and I order a pizza."

T.J. stepped inside and she closed the door behind him.

In the living room, they settled somewhat awkwardly onto the couch, T.J. crossing his arms and Caroline crossing her legs. "Wasn't sure I'd catch you at home," he said for an opener.

"Yeah . . ." Caroline didn't make excuses. Instead she tossed the ball back to him. "What about you? Why aren't you out with *Sandy*?"

T.J. studied her, his green eyes sifting through her tone. Caroline herself wasn't sure if she was teasing or serious.

"Sandy?" He shrugged. "I'm lukewarm about her basically." His eyes didn't let go of her; she had to keep on looking into them. "Discovered there's no potential there."

"Hmm." Caro knew what he was getting at. *You're about as subtle as a bulldozer, McAllister.* Tonight, however, she didn't have a comeback. She wasn't up to double-talk. "I was just about to make some popcorn. Here, find a movie—I'll be back in a minute."

In the kitchen, Caroline started a bag of microwave popcorn, then planted her elbows on the counter and buried her face in her hands. *Gotta get rid of him somehow.* The popcorn started heating up; she listened to the kernels ricocheting around in the bag. Nothing for it but to keep up the cheerful charade. She'd just act tired. T.J. would get the hint after a while and leave.

Caroline piled up a tray with munchies—the popcorn, a package of Oreos, some sodas—figuring if she was chewing constantly she wouldn't have to talk. T.J. shook his head at the junk food feast. "I don't know, Caro. You pack all that away, you're gonna have to start watching your figure." She smiled wryly. *If you only knew . . .*

T.J. had arranged himself full length on the sofa so that she didn't have a choice—she had to stretch out next to him. One of his arms fit snugly around her shoulders; with his free hand he felt around for the popcorn bowl. She moved it within reach, stuffing a handful in her own mouth at the same time.

She ate popcorn, at least half the bowl. The crunching didn't stop her chin from quivering, though. Maybe if T.J. hadn't touched her. If he'd kept his distance, she could've pulled it off. Instead, his body warm behind hers made Caroline ache with unshed tears and unspoken words. Why hadn't she just been satisfied with T.J., his friendship and his love? Why had she gone on wasting herself on other guys?

T.J. must have felt her tremble. He shifted, turning her toward him. He frowned at the tears in her eyes. "It can't be the movie," he joked. "Eddie Murphy isn't supposed to make people cry."

Caro's tears came faster; she couldn't stop them now. Bending her head, she pressed her face against T.J.'s chest. *Don't ask,* she prayed. *Just let me cry.*

"Caro, what is it?" His voice was rough with worry, and his hands, gripping her shoulders to give her a shake were rough, too. "Will you tell me what's bothering you, for once?"

She took a deep breath, part sob, part hiccup. Before she knew what she was saying, the words were out. "You really want to know?" T.J.'s surprised expression and a mountain of jumbled emotions—fear, anger, desperation, loneliness—pushed her on and made her talk. "Okay, here it is. I'm knocked up, *pregnant.* How d'you like that?"

They were sitting up now staring at each other, their faces only inches apart. At Caroline's bald announcement, T.J.'s eyes grew wide and blank. Caro thought he looked like he'd just been hit in the forehead with a hockey puck and hadn't had time to black out yet. *He's never going to talk to me again,* she guessed as he remained shocked and silent. *He's going to walk out of here without a word.*

Not quite. "How . . . ?" T.J. croaked.

"How do you think?" Caroline snapped sarcastically. She looked away from him. She couldn't bear to see disgust in his face. "It was an immaculate conception. I'm the Virgin Mary. How do you think!" She gulped a shaky, hysterical breath. "Don't worry. It's not yours." She tried to laugh. "Now that really *would* be a miracle!"

There was a long moment's agonizing pause. Finally, Caroline couldn't stand it. She had to look at him—she had to know what he thought of her. She turned her tear-streaked face back to his. T.J. was red—blushing? And his lips were pressed together in something that wasn't exactly a frown, but sure as hell wasn't an understanding smile either. He looked embarrassed and uncomfortable.

Then, as his eyes moved over her face, reading it the way he always did, his expression softened and he just looked sad. Without saying anything, he wrapped his arms around her and held her as tightly as he could. Relief washed over Caroline, a relief so intense it bordered on joy. He hadn't rejected her . . . at least not yet.

In the temporary safety of T.J.'s arms, she started to cry again, this time letting out all the stops. T.J. rocked her, stroking her hair with one hand. To Caroline, the world felt like a deep, vast, storm-tossed ocean. She'd be drowning if she didn't have him to hold onto. What would she do if he decided to cut her loose?

NINE

Mr. and Mrs. Hickham and the half-brats stood at the front door poised to go out and dressed in their holiday best, looking like a cut-out paper doll family.

Josh's father made one last mechanical attempt to get Josh and Jason to accompany them. "Sure you two don't want to come?"

Josh made the standard foolproof excuse. "I got a ton of homework . . ."

Jason waved cheerfully. "Go on, you guys. Have a good time!"

The brothers had an instant to enjoy their stepmother's sour, offended scowl before she pushed her bedecked little darlings outside, and Mr. Hickham shut the door behind them.

"Man, there's something to be thankful for," exulted Jason. "We don't have to suffer through Thanksgiving dinner at Audrey's folks' house."

"Nothing could be more grim," agreed Josh, also exhilarated by the narrow escape.

"So let's celebrate." Jason lunged for the T.V. in the living room, switching it on to a football game, the volume at full blast. "What're we going to do for a Thanksgiving feast, though?"

Josh trailed Jason into the kitchen. His head in the fridge, Jason gave a shout of triumph. "Mrs. Smith's frozen pumpkin pie—microwavable!" Pulling out the box, he tossed it to Josh, who removed the pie and started it radiating. When Josh looked up next, Jason was flipping a cold can of beer in his direction.

Josh fielded the beer and popped the top. Jason downed about half of his in one swallow. "Happy Thanksgiving, Jughead," he toasted, knocking his can against Josh's.

"Huh," Josh grunted.

"Hey, where's your enthusiasm, Jughead?" Jason asked cheerfully. "Don't tell me you're wishing you went to eat turkey with the turkeys after all."

Josh took a mouthful of beer and swirled it around with his tongue. Then he shook his head. Of course he didn't wish that. Of course this was the way he wanted to spend Thanksgiving—hanging out with his brother, just the two of them at last. If only he could shake the feeling that the only reason Jason was sticking around was because it was a holiday and the bars were closed.

"Maybe this family isn't the Brady Bunch, but we still got a lot to be thankful for," Jason said suddenly. "I got a lot to be thankful for." He laughed. "Listen to me. What a sap."

In a split second, Josh forgave his brother for blowing him off all that week, because he was feeling the exact same way. If it weren't so corny, he'd have said that what he was thankful for was having his brother home, even for just five minutes here and there.

Josh studied his beer can; Jason read the list of ingredients on the pie box. Then of one accord, they burst into motion. Jason sprinted back towards the living room, yelling as he went. Grabbing the old football Jason had unearthed in the garage and smuggled indoors, Josh spiralled it to his brother. Jason caught it with one arm, preserving his beer but knocking over a lamp in the process.

Brandishing the football over his head, Jason did an end-zone touchdown dance. "It's a Cinderella story," he proclaimed. "The underdogs, down at the half, and they've come back to win it all."

He threw the ball to Josh and then dove on him, tackling him onto the couch in an explosion of doilies and cushions. Josh's beer can went flying. He got the wind knocked out of him, but even so he couldn't help laughing. He couldn't *stop* laughing.

Jason's expression suddenly changed. The microwave buzzer had sounded. "Food! I shall return."

Josh sat up and bent over, his elbows on his knees. The laugh attack passed and he hunted for the spilled beer, which he mopped up with a doily. Then he balled the doily up and shoved it into a particularly hideous vase next to the fireplace.

He flopped back on the couch, waiting for Jason. A feeling of content filled him up. This was going to be his day with Jason. No point resenting the days that had already passed. Having the house to themselves was like heaven. It made Josh feel light-headed. His brother had totally shed his military manner—he seemed to be getting younger and younger. Today, Jason could almost be the seventeen-year-old, the one who was still in high school. The good old days, before Jason left for the service. . . . But they couldn't keep going back in time. Jason left then; he'd be leaving again in a couple days. Josh squeezed the thought out of his mind.

Jason reappeared with a couple more beers, the pie, and two forks. "This is gonna be good," he predicted, digging in. Josh applied his fork, too. They munched inelegantly, lazy eyes turned to the game on the T.V.

About halfway through the pie, Josh realized that this was the moment. He and Jason might not have another chance to talk alone.

Jason apparently had the same idea. He cleared his throat. "I know I've been running around a lot the last couple days, Jug. And dragging you to the bar the other night—couldn't bring this up there. Just wanted to say I know it must've been tough for you, Dad's stroke and all."

"Hmmm," Josh mumbled. *Tough for you* . . . His brother didn't know the half of it. Josh knew the Witch hadn't exactly sent Jason a telegram telling him she'd blamed Josh for Mr. Hickham's stroke and Josh had run away.

"I mean, he's not the world's greatest dad, but he's better than nothing," Jason went on. "It was a pretty close call, huh?"

"I guess."

"Did he just keel over at work or what?"

Had his dad just keeled over or were there warning symptoms? Josh had no idea. "Sort of," he said vaguely.

"What'd they do for him at the hospital? Was he out of it for long?"

Josh shrugged. "I don't really know."

"Must've been worse than I thought, Jug. Sounds like you were really shell-shocked—you weren't all there."

"I wasn't all there," Josh admitted quietly. "I wasn't there at all."

Jason stared at him. "What do you mean?"

"I mean, I wasn't there." Josh spun the tin pie plate onto the coffee table. "I was . . . away."

"Away where?"

Getting the words out was awkward, but also a relief. Josh had wanted to spill this story bad. "I left town for a couple days," he began.

"Left town . . . I don't get it. Where—why?"

"Philadelphia. It just got to be too much for me all of a sudden." Josh looked at the T.V. instead of at Jason. "I couldn't take it anymore. The Witch . . . Dad. Me. Like, I was just so fed up with trying to figure things out and not getting any help, just getting a kick in the face every time I thought I was getting somewhere. And when the Witch called and said Dad had had a stroke and was probably going to die and it was my fault—"

Jason's eyebrows shot together. "She said that?"

Josh shrugged. He couldn't get mad about it himself anymore, although talking about it on top of eating too much pie was making him feel sick. The feeling of loneliness, abandonment—how much he'd needed his brother. . . . "Yeah, well, Dad didn't die, so all's well, you know?"

Jason shook his head. "What a bitch. God, I can't

believe I didn't know about this. So you left town. What in hell were you planning to do?"

"I didn't *plan* anything," Josh answered. "It just happened. I guess I figured since school was pointless, dropping out'd be no great loss. I could get a job somewhere and keep the money I made instead of turning it over to *her*. And maybe someplace totally new I could start over at figuring out what I wanted to do. Who I wanted to be."

Jason touched Josh's arm with his beer can. "But you came back."

"Yeah." Josh tipped his own beer. "I got a couple reasons to stick around for a while longer. Till the school year's out and I graduate, anyway."

Jason was silent for a long moment. "I can't believe I didn't know," he repeated finally. "I would've . . . God. Poor Jughead."

The shocked sympathy in his brother's voice made Josh's eyes sting. He clenched his teeth to kept from blubbering.

"So, what's been pulling you through?" asked Jason. "You still scribbling?"

Josh thought about the life drawing class he was taking at Norwell, the difference it had made. He flicked a glance at his brother. Would Jason think it was stupid, the way his father and stepmother did? "There're some people," he said instead, sidestepping the art question. "Friends. And you, right?"

"Damn straight."

Josh shrugged. "I don't know. Maybe I'm back where I started. I mean, I know more than ever that I want to get out of Redmond and be on my own. But doing what?" Jason didn't answer so Josh filled in the blank. "Maybe a couple years at sea is what I need to set me straight. That's what Dad and the Witch think, anyhow."

He'd tossed the ball to his brother—now it was Jason's turn to offer him the wisdom of the world. Josh looked at him expectantly.

Jason didn't clap him on the shoulder and welcome him to the fraternity. Instead he shook his head, then lifted his can and drained it. "I know how you feel, Jughead. Man, do you ever outgrow it? I'm up in the air about my life, too. One of the reasons I'm not dealing with Dad—the bar's safer."

Josh didn't get it. "What d'you mean?"

"The damn Navy," Jason said. His bitterness and dissatisfaction would've been hard to miss. "Dad pushed it and I used it, you know? So maybe I shouldn't complain if it's using me. I used it as an easy way out of Redmond. Now I've been there two and a half years and I'm starting to think I took a major wrong turn."

"But—"

"It doesn't help you figure out who you are, Jughead," Jason continued, a hard, abstract expression in his eyes. "It makes you somebody. The problem is, it doesn't necessarily make you the somebody you want to be. It's not a doorway, it's a trap."

Jason finished his beer and crumpled the can in his fist. "Everything all day long's figured out to the goddamn millisecond, Jug. What time you wake up, when you eat, when you take a crap. Yeah, they say it builds character. All I know is, seeing the guys again . . . The real world's not perfect. Hell, we all know Redmond's a hole. But compared to the Service? Freedom's relative, man."

Josh was baffled. "But what would you do instead?"

"That's the big question, isn't it?"

Josh stared as Jason threw the mangled can into the fireplace and took off into the kitchen for another beer. The bottom had just dropped out of the universe. His head couldn't take it. He couldn't digest his brother's disillusionment—his own disillusionment.

Josh recognized it now. Ever since he'd come home on leave, Jason had been running away, as bad as Josh ever did. *Wait a minute*, Josh thought. *I'm the kid brother*. Jason was supposed to pave the way. He was supposed to have the answers, the strong arm to lean on.

Instead, all Josh could see was that Jason wasn't there for him—once again.

It was an even more nauseating scene than usual. Suzi had decided to play domestic all of a sudden— she was attempting to roast a Thanksgiving turkey. Meanwhile she and Caro's father had already downed so many Bloody Marys they could barely read the meat thermometer.

Even overlooking the distinct possibility of food poisoning, Caroline didn't feel like hanging around. Her dad and Suzi didn't need her—the two of them made their own party. Their company never was Caroline's idea of a good time and somehow on Thanksgiving, national Happy Family Day, it was even more depressing than usual.

She jingled her car keys as she passed the kitchen on her way out. Not that she *wanted* them to look up, ask her where she was going. Which was a good thing, because they didn't.

The Mustang was the only shiny thing about the day. She'd taken it to the car wash yesterday, gotten an inside/outside job, hot wax, the works. *My baby*, Caroline thought fondly, smoothing her hand across the hood as she walked around to the driver's seat. Then she bit her lip. Maybe the car wasn't the only thing she was going to be taking care of in a while. . . .

For once, Caroline was hungry. Driving north, away from town and into farm country, she thought that turkey actually would've tasted good. She could be eating some right now, and not Suzi's Butterball bomb. T.J. had invited her to have dinner with him and his parents, but she'd turned him down and now she was glad she had. There was no way she could have posed at the table with them, making small talk and acting like she was into the homey family routine. Even in her best moods, that wasn't her scene. T.J. had talked her into a compromise, though; she was going to stop by for dessert later in the afternoon.

Maybe that's why I'm so antsy, Caroline thought, suddenly noticing she was doing eighty and hoping the cops didn't set speed traps on holidays. She had to face it. She was nervous. She and T.J. hadn't really talked since last Saturday night and the Big Confession. Caroline had basically cried herself to sleep; T.J. tucked her into bed and then left. They'd hung out a little at school like usual, but Caroline scrupulously avoided being alone with him. She couldn't remember the last time she'd swung by Split River Station.

Meanwhile T.J. hadn't exactly been beating down her door. He'd only called once since Saturday, yesterday to invite her over for Thanksgiving dinner. She knew what *her* thoughts were all about these days. What was going on in T.J.'s head?

As she drove, Caroline scanned the fields blurring by, absorbing colors—brown, grey, gold—rather than shapes. *T.J.'s judging me*, she decided, recalling his remarks and moods and the quality of his glance during the past five days. He was judging her, and she was scared to hear the verdict. At least he hadn't totally blown her off. Maybe it was just a matter of time. The more he thought about the situation, the more it had to bother him. Caroline tried to put herself in his shoes and imagine herself a guy, in love, sort of, with a girl who was pregnant with somebody else's baby. Would she say, "You've made your bed, now lie on it," and go on her way?

Caroline rubbed her eyes with the back of her wrist, determined not to let the tears start. She'd never had sympathy for girls who cried their way through life; she was sick of herself for being so emotional these days. *The road. Just keep your eyes on the road.*

It wasn't the first time she'd wanted to keep on driving and never turn back. Maybe Josh had the right idea last month, running away. She could head for the city—empty her bank account first, not take off half-assed like Josh did—get a job, have the kid. She wouldn't be the only unwed mother there.

So far she hadn't even gotten out of Redmond. Caroline realized she'd ditched the main highway for a back road that cut through some of the more prosperous farms in the area. Brad Gradowski's family lived out this way, and Jeanette Miller, or rather Jeanette Parsons. She'd been a year ahead of Caroline in school—one of the few Norwell High girls Caro could stand. They'd partied together back when Caro was dating Brad a year and a half ago. Not long after that Jeanette had dropped out of school and had a baby. Married the guy, a nice Brad-style farmboy type, Chuck Parsons. Caroline hadn't seen her since then.

She knew which house was Jeanette and Chuck's; it was just a couple down from the Gradowskis'. Caroline turned down the road, suddenly curious. There it was: "Parsons" in red block letters on the mailbox. She slowed the Mustang, feeling a little bit cheesy, like the kind of person who drove by movie stars' homes trying to spy in the windows. She couldn't help it, though. She couldn't help wondering.

Were Jeanette and Chuck and the baby having a little Thanksgiving dinner? Were Jeanette and Chuck happy, or did they hate each other? Most of all Caroline wondered, since in her case a husband didn't figure into the picture, what was it like to be eighteen and a mother?

There were ruffled curtains in the front kitchen windows. The lights were on—the house had a soft glow in the grey November afternoon—but it didn't tell Caroline anything. It didn't answer her questions.

TEN

"Great bird, Mom. Don't know when you've cooked a better one."

"Really? You're sure not eating much of it," Mrs. McAllister pointed out.

T.J. looked down at his plate. True. It was still piled foolishly high with mashed potatoes, neon-orange squash, green beans, and about half a turkey. He'd taken a couple bites so he could compliment his mom without being a total hypocrite, but for some reason chewing and swallowing just wasn't coming easy to him today.

"It's just it's so good," he swore, seizing his fork as if to make a move on the meal. "I'm prolonging the ecstasy."

His mother gave him one of those "right, tell me about it" looks. She saw right through him; she often did. He ought to know better by now. You couldn't out-McAllister a McAllister.

She didn't butt in, though. "Well, I think it's pretty good," she declared.

T.J.'s dad nodded enthusiastically, a mouthful preventing him from singing the turkey's praises.

Determinedly, T.J. pushed at the potatoes and squash with his fork. By compressing them into a mound camouflaged by green beans, he was able to create the illusion of a half-empty plate. This accomplished, he shoved back his chair. "Mind if I excuse myself?"

He knew he could count on his parents being cool. They respected the privacy of his soul; when he didn't offer an explanation, they didn't ask for one. "Come down later for pie," was all his mother said.

As he escaped the dining room, they were already starting in on a conversation about work, or rather the usual debate about whose job was the most thankless. Upstairs, T.J. went right for his stereo. He slipped in a Stones cassette and blasted it, as loud as he thought he could get away with without bringing one of his parents to the bottom of the stairs shouting at him to turn it down.

He flopped backwards on his bed, arms folded behind his head. The music was supposed to drown out his thoughts, the thoughts that wouldn't let him eat Thanksgiving dinner. It succeeded, sort of. At least, it broke the thoughts into pieces, made a kaleidoscope out of his brain.

No good. He had to deal with his thoughts, view them whole. Caroline's body was changing with every passing minute—he didn't have time to mess around. He turned the volume down.

Not that she'd *asked* for his advice. He thought back on the scene the other night. Never had all the contradictions of Caroline's personality come across so clearly: her vulnerability, her isolation, her need, her defiance. The shock of it came back to T.J. with barely abated force. Caro's angry, defensive tone—his jaw-dropping act. He squeezed the nerf ball he'd been bouncing against the wall, squeezed it the way he felt like his brain or heart or guts or wherever a person's emotions sprang from was being squeezed these days. T.J. went red in the face, just remembering the way he'd felt at that instant. Like, it hadn't been fair. It was the last thing in the world he'd expected her to say. He was caught so off guard, it wasn't even funny.

He rolled over on the bed, burying his face in the pillow to keep himself from hollering. It was idiotic, but he couldn't help it—he actually felt *cheated* on. Not that he'd been in the dark about her social life. Caroline Buchanan had always done exactly as she pleased.

But getting *pregnant*. Caroline, having sex with another guy—who was it anyway, that Brad what's-his-name with the farmer muscles and the pick-up truck?

Not my business, T.J. reminded himself sternly. *My business is to help her, not judge her*. Or was it? How could he help judging? He loved her and she knew it. He had to be partly jealous and mad. He also had to get beyond those feelings. Get beyond them . . . to where?

She hadn't asked for his opinion, but she was waiting for him to respond. All week, she'd kept her distance and let him keep his. But in an hour or so, the distance was going to dissolve. She'd be here, they'd be together. And he had to be ready to tell her what he thought.

T.J. sat up. On the foot of the bed was a jumble of library books, the novels he still had to plow through for the upcoming scholarship test. He kicked them off the bed, maliciously enjoying the sound they made falling on the floor with a crunch of crumpling pages.

She cared for him. That was a given. If she didn't, it wouldn't have hurt her to tell him. She wouldn't have told him at all. But did she care as much as he did? Her being pregnant with somebody else's baby had to mean something. What, though, T.J. didn't know. He just knew that, despite the hurt, he loved her. She was still the only person in the world that turned him on, made him want to do it all, made him feel he could. He'd die for her. He'd be pregnant in her place if he could.

T.J. yanked the bottom drawer out from the old wooden desk where he'd stowed his top-secret stuff since he was old enough to *have* top-secret stuff. Pulled a paperback book out from under a bunch of letters, and had to laugh at himself. It was a switch from the old days when he was hiding *Playboy* magazines and other such adolescent reading material.

Your basic how-to. How to have a baby. Diet and exercise and medical care for the pregnant woman. What to have on hand when you got home from the hospital with the new bundle of joy. Breast-feeding, teething, diapers, strollers. With this step-by-step guide, anybody could do it.

T.J. thought about his parents sitting downstairs, totally oblivious. He thought about high school and the scholarship contest and college . . . and Caro.

*   *   *

When she pulled up the McAllisters' driveway in
the Mustang, he was ready. Caroline didn't even
have time to let the engine die; T.J. hopped right in
the passenger side. "Pie to go," he explained,
exhibiting a foil-wrapped wedge.

She shifted into reverse and laughed. "You hiding me from your parents?"

Half-kidding, half-serious. The balance was so
fine. T.J. didn't want to tip it, so he kept straight.
"Naw. Just thought I'd spare you the small talk.
Basically, I was looking for an excuse to eat this with
my fingers like a caveman."

The atmosphere between them was colored by
what Caroline had said the other day and all they
had yet to say to each other, but the tension factor
wasn't as bad as T.J. had expected. *Should've
figured*, he thought. Caro was tougher, more invulnerable when she was in her car. Behind the
wheel of the Mustang, all that was gentle and young
and scared in her stayed securely under wraps.

She didn't ask him where he wanted to go; she
just went. T.J. wasn't surprised when they ended
up in the Nob Hill part of town at the turn-out by
the waterfall. It was a private, hidden place—it fit
the feeling.

The day was warmish for November. The rock
ledge over the falls was baking mildly in the
mid-afternoon sun; they didn't need the blanket
Caro brought from the car.

Sitting side by side, they looked down at the
rushing, glinting water instead of at each other.
Caro broke the silence. "Wasn't sure you were ever

going to talk to me again." Once more there was a half-kidding, half-serious twist in her low, husky voice.

Tin foil crinkling, T.J. unwrapped the pie. "You'll never shake me off," he assured her. "Pecan or apple? Me and Dad were in charge of the pies, and since we couldn't decide which we liked better we made both."

Caroline shrugged. "I don't care. Pecan."

T.J. held out the piece of pie, then on second thought withdrew it. "Maybe you should have the apple," he said. "Pecan has a ton of sugar in it. The fruit would be better for you."

A blank stare from Caro. *Remove foot from mouth*. T.J. handed her the pecan pie and some foil for a plate. She rested it on one outstretched knee. And waited. The line of her beautiful profile spoke volumes to him. Aloof, needy, brave, wistful.

Putting out a hand, T.J. touched Caroline's face. She rested her cheek against his hand, briefly. Then straightened again, still waiting.

"You know . . ." T.J. proceeded cautiously, knowing he was walking on hot coals. "There are a couple of . . . options."

The eyes Caroline turned on him were as grey and cold as the water of the river below. "You mean like an abortion?" she said bluntly, her voice cracking on the word. "Yeah, I know about my *options*. I talked to a counselor at the clinic."

T.J. didn't let himself falter in the face of Caroline's pain. He had to be honest with her. "Abortion's one of them. But it's not what I was thinking."

She still didn't cut him any slack. "Let me in on it. What *were* you thinking?"

This time he stuttered a little, but he got the words out. "We—we could have the baby."

"*We?*" Caroline snapped. She crumpled the tin foil around the untouched piece of pie and tossed the whole thing down into the river. "*We* could have the baby?" Her voice rose. "You mean *I* could have it. I could—me. I'm the one who's pregnant. It's my problem. Is that what you're telling me?"

"No, it's not." T.J.'s mouth was dry and his palms were wet. He couldn't believe he was about to say what he was about to say. Maybe she'd laugh in his face. He wasn't even her lover, not like that other guy who remained nameless. *Will she want this? Will she want me?* He couldn't know unless he asked. "What I meant to say was, we could have the baby—together. We could get married."

T.J. held his breath. Caroline's eyes went wide and round, then she tipped her head back and laughed. "People don't do that anymore, Mc-Allister," she said, her sarcasm making him feel small. "Anyway, you don't have anything to worry about. My dad's not coming after *you* with a shotgun—you're not the one that knocked me up. Not that the old man would care if he knew, which he doesn't and won't."

She was on a roll, careless and defiant, and it hurt him, just the way he knew she meant it to. Hard as nails, always. For a second, it threw T.J. off. *Maybe I made a bad call. I've got her wrong, all wrong.*

But as the words, her tone, sank deeper into his soul, he felt what was underneath them. A dare:

Tell me you really mean it. She didn't want him to be passive, to humor her.

He grabbed her shoulders and shook her hard, making her meet his eyes. "Wake up, Caro," he shouted. "The old 'I'm tough, I can take it on the chin' act isn't going to work. Do you think this is easy for me, some kind of joke? Do you think you're the only one that has feelings?"

Caroline dropped her gaze. Slowly, she shook her head.

"It's not a joke. We ain't in any old comic strip. I'm not Superman, and you're sure as hell not Lois Lane." He saw the shadow of a smile on her face. "I want to be with you on this, Caro," T.J. said, his voice soft and sure now. "You need me. You got me."

Caro remained still and quiet; T.J. knew he'd hit a chord. He relaxed his grip on her shoulders. Sliding his hands around her back, he pulled her close to him, feeling that never again would they hold each other at arm's length. "Caroline."

She looked up at his solemn tone. T.J. studied her face and suddenly he got scared again. She was so close, so *real*. The situation was so real. The step he was about to take—once he took it, there was no going back. By joining his fate with Caro's, his own life would change drastically, forever.

But he was ready. After months of holding back, he was ready. He took the step. "I love you, Caro. When I first met you, I knew I wanted to spend the rest of my life with you. It was just a question of when 'the rest of my life' was going to start. I'm willing to make it now if you are."

When she remained silent, he continued. "I just

want you to know . . . you have to believe . . . whatever you decide to do about the pregnancy, I'll support you. If you want to keep it, well, maybe I'm not the real father, but that doesn't matter to me. I want to be a family with you."

The soft curve of the shadow-smile deepened. Through the sparkle of tears, T.J. could see the recognition in her eyes. "I love you, too," she whispered.

Maybe it wasn't an answer, but it was a beginning.

ELEVEN

"Ex-cuuuse *me*," a super scumbag in a motor-oiled leather jacket said to Caroline as she bumped against him in the packed hall at Norwell on Monday morning. She didn't waste a glance on him but kept on knifing through the crowd in the direction of her French class. She was not psyched to be back at school after the long Thanksgiving weekend. It was reality, though, she had to admit to herself.

And as such, a stark contrast to the conversation she and T.J. had a few days ago about getting married. Sitting there on the rock over the falls, she'd been bewitched into thinking it was a possibility. Here in the halls of Nowhere High, the whole scheme seemed ridiculous. What came over them to even discuss such an idea? Maybe they loved each other, but when you really thought about it, love didn't have all that much to do with it. Getting married wasn't like playing house—she and T.J. couldn't just install a bassinet at the old train station. Being parents was for real, or at least it was supposed to be. Caroline thought about her own parents. They failed at their marriage; her own mom abandoned her. Not a great precedent.

Her focus shifted from inside to outside, and she studied the faces of the kids pushing past her. Good-looking, plain, white, black, angry, bored, dreamy, rebellious. And young—damn, they all looked so young, despite the fact that most of them wore whatever clothes and makeup and behavior they thought would help them seem older. She imagined what they were all thinking about and figured she could compile a ranked list: sex; their appearance, which led back to sex again; and maybe lunch, which was coming up in another hour. *What makes me and T.J. think we're any different?* Caroline wondered, snagging an empty seat in the back row of her French classroom. *Goofy seventeen-year-old T.J., and me who goes nuts if I spend too much time in the same place. With a baby. Mom and Pops.*

"Tennis after school?" Darcy dumped her books on the next desk.

Caroline considered making an excuse, which she'd been doing a lot lately, then thought, *what the hell.* She needed the exercise, and maybe if she didn't give in to feeling tired, she wouldn't be. "You're on," she replied.

"It's pretty warm today," said Darcy. "Want to try the outdoor courts one last time?"

"Sure. I'm up for it."

Class got underway. Caroline copied the irregular verbs Mr. Kincaid was writing on the blackboard, but they didn't have any meaning for her.

French—talk about a stupid thing to be wasting brain cells on. *Gonna be real useful to me in the future . . . unless I go to Paris to have the baby.*

Her pen wandered to the margin of her notebook and she doodled, drawing little bubbles. Starting small, the bubbles grew bigger and bigger and rounder and rounder . . . She drew an "X" through them and dropped her pen. Wishing she didn't have to keep thinking about the same old thing, didn't have to make a *decision*. She did, though. It was still early, but the more time passed, the harder it would be to go through with an abortion.

As Mr. Kincaid asked some butt-kisser in the front row to read aloud, Caroline examined the idea in her head. Abortion. She was for it, in theory. Maybe she didn't always treat her body well, but it was *her* body, her self, and nobody but her had a right to say what she should do with it.

She could go to the clinic and have the abortion. From everything she'd heard, it was a pretty simple procedure—you were in and out in a couple of hours. Then she'd be herself again, just herself, Caroline Buchanan, with no trespasser in her belly. She could start over, and let T.J. off the hook. She'd get her life back.

Her life . . . that was the problem. She was already sharing her life with this baby. *But what right do I have to bring a kid that I don't even want into the world? I couldn't give it a decent home—I don't even know if I could love it.*

Whenever she thought about actually having an abortion, though, Caroline got shaky. She was shaky

now, and suddenly nauseous. *God, please. Don't
make me have to bolt for the bathroom.*

She closed her eyes until it passed, then shot a
quick glance at Darcy. Nope, her friend hadn't
noticed the near barf attack. Caroline sighed. She
almost wished Darcy *had* noticed, had asked,
"What's wrong?"

Someone to talk to. . . . Not T.J., not Maribeth at the clinic. Maybe if she had a mom, the
kind of mom she'd like to be herself someday, the
kind a kid could talk to. But she didn't. She'd had
the other kind of mom, the kind who didn't even
like her own kid enough to want to live with her.

Darcy paid for her lunch and then stared into the
Dante's Inferno that was the Nowhere High cafeteria. Bodies everywhere, and she still didn't
know—didn't want to know—most of them. Where
were Caro and Alison?

The old I-don't-belong-here feeling twisted the
hunger out of Darcy's stomach. Ernest Norwell
High School wasn't Sesame Street; you couldn't just
plop down at any old table and make instant
friends. Darcy had learned fast that the Caros and
Alisons were rare; nastiness prevailed.

She was about to stick her sandwich in her
shoulder bag and eat it in the library, as she had on
more than one previous occasion, when someone
bumped lightly against her back with his tray.

"Planning to eat standing up or what?"

Darcy turned and looked up at Marc Calamano.
She laughed. "You caught me."

"I see a seat for you." He gripped his tray with

one hand and steered her toward a table in jock territory with the other. A bunch of brawny guys and two empty chairs. *Great, me and the football team,* Darcy thought.

"Know everybody, Darce?"

"Not even close," she confessed.

"Do the honors, Calamano," one of the guys suggested.

"Bart, Charlie, Greg, Phil—this is Darcy Jenner."

"Hey." She waved. "It's a pleasure."

"So, keep it clean," said Marc. "There's a lady in the locker room now."

"Man, you spoiled all our fun," Greg joked. "We were just about to hold a farting contest."

Darcy bit into her sandwich. *Looks like this is going to be an elevating lunch hour.*

Marc put a hand on her shoulder. "You don't have to talk to these losers," he assured her. "You can talk to me instead. Been to the station lately?"

"Can't remember the last time I hung out there. Too cold."

"Yeah. Cold." Then he laughed and Darcy blushed, wondering if he was thinking about the times he and Alison got hot there.

He must have been thinking something like that. "She happy with Hickham?"

Darcy nodded. "Seems to be."

"He's Mr. Sensitive. Yeah, it follows."

Darcy chewed thoughtfully. It was funny. For a while there, it was her with Josh and Alison with Marc. Now Josh and Alison were a pair, and Marc was back chasing cheerleaders. Then there were T.J. and Caro, and Darcy wasn't sure she'd ever understand what was going on there. *Trial by error, baptism by fire—I guess that's the way modern love works*.

Speaking of chasing cheerleaders. Apparently Marc spotted someone who just couldn't wait a few tables down. He pushed back his chair. "Back in a flash," he promised Darcy.

She chewed faster, figuring she'd finish her sandwich and split. She didn't have much to contribute to the sports rap.

"Darcy."

Marc had been sitting on her right; Phil, the one who'd said, "Do the honors," was on her left. Darcy gave him a shy smile. He smiled back and she noticed he was handsome. Not the sort of looks that knocked your socks off, but a nice face. Nice eyes. What was he going to say, though? Something about a farting contest?

"You've just about made it through your first semester at Nowhere High," Phil observed. "They should give you a medal or something."

"I agree," said Darcy. "It was touch and go there for a while. I thought some of the junior class monster women were going to eat me alive."

"Guys are easier on a new girl, no doubt about it," he remarked.

"Ummm." Darcy lowered her eyelashes. She still wasn't used to the way they were "easier." Two years at a girls' boarding school hadn't exactly prepared her for fending off the sharks in a coed fishbowl.

"Hey, don't worry." Phil gave her another smile. "I'm not dealing on you."

Darcy drew a hand across her forehead. "What a relief," she quipped.

"You know what, though? I bet you have nice handwriting."

She lifted her eyebrows.

"Here." Phil ripped a piece of paper out of his notebook. Taking her hand, he slipped a pen in her fingers. "Let's see you write something."

"Like what?"

He grinned. "How about your phone number?"

Darcy laughed but she went ahead and printed the number. Phil took the page and inspected it. "Yep, I was right. Very nice handwriting." He gave the paper back to her.

Darcy tilted her head, puzzled. "Don't you want this?"

"Sure, if you'd like to give it to me," he replied.

She folded the paper in half and presented it to him formally, thinking as she did what a contrast this was to the time she gave her phone number to Nick, the gorgeous badlands guy she'd had a brief, terrifying fling with earlier that fall. She certainly wasn't scared right now, or even excited. Just pleased.

"Mind if I dial this number sometime?" Phil asked, folding the sheet again and slipping it into his pocket.

"Not at all," she said, knowing she'd be disappointed if he didn't.

"So, what's the mystery?" Alison asked, her eyes round with curiosity over the rim of her milkshake. Caroline kidnapped her from the school cafeteria at the beginning of lunch period, without really explaining herself. Now they were in the burger-stand parking lot, a greasy takeout bag on the seat in between them. "Well?" Alison prompted, wondering what could make shoot-from-the-hip Caro act so roundabout.

Caroline bit into her bacon cheeseburger and chewed slowly, as if she were buying herself some time. Then she looked straight at Alison, a strangely confiding but guarded look in her grey-green eyes. "Brace yourself," she said, her tone light.

"I'm braced." Alison smiled expectantly. She was ready for a surprise, figuring it had to be something good. She didn't think Caro would drag out the suspense like this otherwise.

"I'm pregnant."

Alison was about to put a french fry in her mouth. She stopped, her hand still raised and her mouth open. Then she closed her mouth; the french fry dropped on the floor of the car. *Pregnant?* For a second, she thought she'd shouted the word out loud. Then she realized the horrible echo was inside her skull. "T—T.J.?" she stuttered.

Caroline shook her head. Her voice was uneven, too, but she still managed to sound nonchalant. "No. Some other guy."

Alison took a deep breath, trying to see her way through Caroline's devastating news to solid ground. *What do I say?* She couldn't speak; she put a hand on Caroline's arm.

Caroline looked contrite. "Sorry to dump this on you like that."

Alison patted her. "Don't be. I'm glad you told

me," she assured Caro, even though she wasn't glad—she felt like she'd been hit by a car. "You know you can turn to me, any time. But what are you—" She hesitated. "What does he—"

"*He's* got nothing to do with it," Caroline said bluntly. "He's just some guy. I'm not even going to tell him."

This shock was off the Richter scale. Alison stared at Caro in disbelief. "Not tell him? But you have to tell him. He's the—the father." It sounded so personal; Alison felt her cheeks go red. She continued, though. "Caro, he has a right to know."

"He doesn't have a right to anything," Caro declared.

"But he must care for you. He'd want to—"

Caro laughed, stomping effectively on Alison's romantic attitudes. "Caring doesn't have anything to do with it. We slept together because it felt good. It didn't mean anything."

Tears sprang to Alison's eyes. Caroline had always talked so tough. The more she hurt, Alison knew, the harder she hit. This confession couldn't be easy for her. Caro, who had such a hard time trusting people. *She's come to me for help; I can't let her down.*

Alison couldn't lie to her either. "It did mean something," she whispered, "whether you believe it or not. It . . . it created something."

"He's nothing to me," Caroline insisted. "Get it?"

Alison sank back against the seat, feeling wounded and stupid. "I know I'm saying all the wrong things," she mumbled. "I'm sorry."

The impatient scowl dissolved. "Oh, Mouse. *I'm* sorry. I know it's probably hard for you to understand. You have to take my word for it."

"I can do that," Alison said, determined not to let on that she thought it was sad. Caro needed strength, not pity. With a pang, Alison recognized something. It *was* sad—and it could've been *her*. She and Marc had made love, and she thought it meant forever, but it didn't. If she'd gotten pregnant, would Marc have married her or dumped her? Would she have been forced to say to the world, "He's nothing to me"?

For a moment they munched in silence. "Shouldn't be eating this junk," Caroline observed. "T.J. was fussing at me about sugar and stuff."

"You told T.J.?"

"Yeah." Caroline's smile was weary. "He kind of flipped at first. Who could blame him, right? But then . . ." She paused and, as Alison watched, her expression grew soft and young and hopeful. "You'll never believe what he came out with the other day." Caro laughed. "He actually asked me to marry him. Marry him, and have the baby."

Alison gaped. "You're kidding."

"Nope. He wasn't being corny and idealistic, though," Caroline added, her tone thoughtful. "I guess we finally figured out that we . . . love each other. Maybe we *could* put up with each other for the rest of our lives."

She's serious, Alison realized. *They're serious.* "You mean you're really thinking about it?"

"Maybe the best option I've got."

The french fries were cold, but for a minute Alison kept eating them. Then she said slowly, "You and T.J. have something special. But a baby already on the way . . . that's a hard way to start a marriage."

Caroline sighed. Her face was averted, hidden from Alison by a curtain of silvery brown hair. Now she lifted it in order to look her friend straight in the eye. "But if it was you, would *you* have an abortion?"

Tears brimming again, Alison shook her head. She didn't have to think twice. "No." she declared. "I could never kill a baby that was growing inside me. Never."

Caroline put her hands to her face, but not before Alison saw the anguish there. *That was the worst thing I could have said,* she realized remorsefully. But it was also the only thing. It was the way she felt, and she didn't think her friend should hide from what she believed abortion really involved.

Taking one of Caro's hands, Alison squeezed it tightly. "Maybe you need to talk to someone else," she said, knowing she sounded wimpy and weak. This was over her head, though. Caro needed more help than she could give.

Caroline shrugged. "Like who? You and T.J. are the only ones I trust—you and the people at the clinic. Who else could possibly have an opinion?"

"I don't know. Maybe somebody who's been through the same thing, you know? I mean, not just a professional opinion like at the clinic. A girl who got pregnant and had the baby and maybe got married." Alison had never felt so helpless and inexperienced. "I don't know," she repeated.

To Alison's surprise, Caroline didn't brush off the suggestion. Instead, her sea-green eyes registered some kind of a connection. She put her hand to the key in the ignition and the Mustang's engine grumbled to life. "Will you come with me to see somebody?"

TWELVE

Driving through the badlands toward Jeanette's part of town, Caroline started having second thoughts. What was she doing? She couldn't just barge into Jeanette's life and pick her brains. She couldn't *pry*. It went against all her instincts.

Alison had gotten through to her with that last comment, though. Caro had looked everywhere for an answer. Talking to Jeanette, seeing for herself— maybe this would help her figure things out.

Caroline glanced at Alison, feeling a gratitude tinged with guilt. She could have just told Alison she was pregnant, cried on her shoulder, and all that. Instead, she'd used her as a sounding board and bashed her around a bit. Gentle little Mouse.

"Sure you don't mind skipping class?" Caroline asked. "I don't want to get you in trouble. It's not too late to turn around and get back to school before lunch ends." *Give me an excuse to chicken out.*

"You're more important to me than trigonometry," said Alison. "But do you want to give me a hint about where we're going?"

"You remember Jeanette Miller from our class? Jeanette Parsons now."

Alison looked blank. "Jeanette Miller from *Brownies*?"

Caro laughed. "Didn't know you'd have to think back *that* far."

"I guess we didn't move in the same circles after that," explained Alison with a smile.

"Well, I haven't seen her in ages—not since she had her baby. She doesn't exactly hang around the strip anymore on Friday nights, you know? But she was a pretty cool girl. I remember being bummed when I heard she got in—" Caroline stopped. Fill in the blank, she thought. *In trouble . . .*

Alison slid right over it. "So, what are you going to say to her?"

Caroline shrugged. "I don't need a script. I'm not going to *say* anything. I just want to *see*."

"Oh."

By the time they turned onto Jeanette and Chuck's road, Caroline was nervous, though. She braked at their mailbox, steering the Mustang off the blacktop. They rumbled to a stop in a billow of dust. For a second, she and Alison just sat there. Then Caroline flung her door open, making the gesture as bold as possible. "Let's go."

A new wimp hope occurred to her—maybe Jeanette wouldn't be home. As she pressed the doorbell, however, she could hear the T.V. blaring inside.

Jeanette opened the door looking suspicious, like she was expecting a pushy salesman or one of those door-to-door religious fanatics. Then her blue eyes brightened with pleasure. "Caro! No way. What are you doing here?"

"Oh, me and Alison—you know Alison Laurel?— we were just in the neighborhood . . ." How dumb did that sound? "Cutting class, you know. Out for a drive. And I saw your mailbox and—"

Jeanette shook her head. "It's been a long time. Come in and have a cup of coffee? I'd love to catch up."

There was no mistaking Jeanette's warmth and sincerity. Caroline relaxed. "Sure. If it's not a bad time . . ."

"Naw. I'm just feeding the little monster. And myself. And, God, sorry for the mess. You know how it is."

They followed Jeanette inside and Caroline took it all in. The cramped but cutely decorated living room, scattered with magazines and baby toys. A soap opera on the T.V., a row of tiny cactuses on the south-facing windowsill, and a couple of art prints and a Miller Beer lamp on the wall. A basket of laundry under the kitchen table, a half-eaten tuna salad sandwich and a can of diet soda on top. *You know how it is. . . .*

"This is Sheri," Jeanette said, nodding toward the chubby-cheeked baby girl in a high chair. "You've got a big birthday coming up next week, don't you, sweetie? One whole year old. I can't believe it."

Alison squatted right down next to the high chair, cooing like a little mother bird. Caroline kept her distance and stared, taking in the silky blond curls, the stained Winnie-the-Pooh bib. Sheri spanked her spaghetti with a midget-sized spoon, bubbling with laughter at the silly faces Alison was making. A funny, warm feeling of sympathetic life fluttered in Caroline's stomach. *She's not just a baby,* she marvelled, *she's a real person.*

"Looks like Chuck, doesn't she?"

Caroline tore her gaze away from Sheri. "She got his coloring. But that's your giggle."

Jeanette laughed as she slid back the tray on the high chair. With sure, strong hands, she extricated Sheri from some sort of seat belt thing and set her on the floor. "She can bawl as good as me, too. Hang around long enough, I'm sure you'll get to hear a sample. Coffee or soda, you guys?"

"Coffee," Caro and Alison said together.

Sheri toddled into the living room with Alison trailing. Caro and Jeanette brought the coffee; the three big people settled on the L-shaped couch.

Caro didn't know what to do now. Luckily Alison wasn't at a loss. "What a doll. She's really cute, Jeanette."

Jeanette tipped her head, considering her daughter. "Isn't she?" Then she grimaced. "Wasn't always, though. Believe me, they're not *born* like this. I mean, at first she was just a *thing.* All she could do was cry and nurse and poop. In that order."

They all laughed. Sheri threw a small cardboard book at Alison, who obliged her by bending over and turning the pages with her.

"I mostly can't wait until she starts talking," Jeanette remarked. "You get kind of tired of monologues, you know?"

"Ummm." Caroline sipped her coffee, imagining. Sitting around the house, talking to a baby who couldn't talk back. Putting on your makeup in the morning for the benefit of somebody who wore diapers. Waiting for your husband to get home so you could actually have a conversation. How strange. She felt strange now. Out of place. The way Mouse would feel, Caroline supposed, trying out for a theater role that just didn't fit.

"So, you have to tell me what's going on out there," Jeanette went on. "Chuck is the most boring news source. All I hear about is the guys at work, like I care."

"Same old Nowhere High," said Caroline. "How come I never see you around town?"

"Oh, Gardner's closer for shopping and stuff. Hey, I've seen Brad a couple times lately. He says you guys go out every now and then."

"Um hmm."

"Yeah, I miss the old days sometimes." Jeanette put her feet up on the coffee table. "Just hanging out, you know? Staying up as late as I want and sleeping as late as I want."

"It gets old after a while," said Caroline.

"But it was easy. Everything was easy back then." Jeanette pulled her long brown ponytail over one shoulder and twisted it. "I can't tell you, Caro. There've been so many times I've thought, 'What the hell'd you do, girl?'"

Caroline laughed sympathetically; Jeanette shook her head. "I mean, Chuck and I are so damn young. It's true, sometimes I feel about forty, but most of the time I still feel young. Too young to be a mom, you know? I know he feels the same way, when he goes to the bar sometimes after work with the guys. Too young to be tied down for life."

This was easier than Caroline thought it would be. She didn't have to prompt Jeanette; Jeanette just talked. *She's lonely*, Caroline realized. "Chuck's wild about you, though. Brad always talks about how whipped and devoted he is."

"I don't know. Sometimes I think he hates me. Because of the pressure, you know? Like, he's the breadwinner. He can't ever miss a day of work, just play hooky. I mean, neither can I. I don't ever get a day off, either." Jeanette shot Sheri a look that was part mother-love, part prisoner-of-war. "I get maybe ten minutes a day, if I'm lucky. When she's down for a nap there's cleaning and laundry and all, and when she's up I have to watch her every minute, especially now that she's walking."

Caroline crossed her arms. All of a sudden she felt cold, queasy, claustrophobic.

"Listen to me. What a downer, huh?" Jeanette sat up straighter, her expression lightening. "Don't get the wrong idea. I wouldn't go back and do it any different."

"You've got a beautiful little girl," said Alison, who was bouncing the baby on her knee with the expertise of somebody who had two younger siblings.

Jeanette nodded. "I know. Life's not one big party anymore, but I've got Sheri, and Chuck, and I'm crazy about both of them. We get by okay. Sometimes even better than okay."

As if on cue, Sheri started bawling. Alison stood up and gingerly handed her over to Jeanette. "I think it's the diaper."

Caroline stood up, too, already edging toward the door. "Hey, Jeanette. We've got to go. Great to see you—thanks for the coffee."

Sheri riding on her hip, Jeanette escorted Caro and Alison to the door. "Anytime. Really. Maybe I'll get a babysitter one of these nights—me and Chuck and you and Brad could go out."

"Sure. So long."

Jeanette waved good-bye from the door; Sheri's relentless crying chased them down the driveway. All the while, Caroline was conscious of the fact that if it were *her* baby, she couldn't run out like this. If Sheri were hers, she'd have to deal with the crying, the diapers, the messy spaghetti. The Mustang would just be for trips to the grocery store and the pediatrician. Suddenly, Nowhere High didn't seem so bad.

"We can make it back in time for last period," Alison said as Caroline hit the gas.

They didn't talk as they drove back towards Redmond. Alison seemed to understand that Caroline needed to be alone with her thoughts. Those thoughts were crazy. *She* was crazy, Caroline decided, for thinking that seeing Jeanette was going to make her decision any easier.

At that moment, Caroline realized something for the first time. Somewhere along the line—since T.J.'s proposal?—she'd accepted the idea of going through with the pregnancy and having the baby. She couldn't abort . . . she just couldn't. The decision had been made.

What she had to deal with now were the consequences of that decision. Having a baby in theory was easier than having one for real, that much was obvious. It looked like it was really work—as much work or more than a nine-to-five job. And the responsibility. A feeling of panic clutched Caroline's guts. *You can't just go cruising when the baby cries*.

She couldn't do what Jeanette had done. Give up her freedom, her youth, once and for all, forever. Not to mention asking T.J. to make the same sacrifice. What if he won that stupid Redmond City Scholarship? What about *his* future? Jeanette said it was worth it, though. *We get by . . .*

But I don't want to just "get by."

She and Mouse walked around the back of the school from the parking lot, going in at the door by the outdoor student smoking lounge where they weren't likely to be bagged by a hall monitor. The bell would be ringing any minute. Alison had Spanish last; Caro had science.

At Alison's locker, they parted. "We can talk again whenever you want, Caro," Alison promised. "I have band practice as usual, but not much else. You know where to find me."

Mouse had really come through for her. Caroline knew she wouldn't have had the guts to stop by Jeanette's on her own. "Thanks, kid."

Feeling a little wired from the tension and the coffee at Jeanette's, Caro went back outside to the smoking lounge. Nobody was out there. It was gray and raw—most people were probably sneaking their cigarettes in the bathroom today. *I could use a smoke myself, and to hell with taking care of my health*.

She didn't usually smoke, and she didn't have change for the machine, so she just sat on a bench and inhaled cold unadulterated air until she felt ready to face science class. School. Life.

"Josh!" Alison's face brightened. "I can't believe you biked over in this. Get inside!"

The gray day had dissolved into a night of freezing rain. Josh stomped his feet on the welcome mat and shook his dripping hair. "Sorry," he said, his teeth chattering. "I'm a mess."

"That's okay," Alison assured him. "Woofer came in a few minutes ago looking worse than you do. Just kick off your shoes. Here, give me your jacket."

She pushed him to the bathroom to towel him off. "I feel like a dog at the beauty parlor," he protested. "Like next you're going to clip my nails and groom me."

"Nope." She handed him a blanket. "Wrap up in this."

Alison stuck her head into the living room where her two younger brothers were watching a dubbed kung-fu movie on T.V. "Woofer, you want to call for a pizza?"

"Mom working tonight?" he asked hopefully.

She laughed. "Yes, so get all the junk on it you want. Order two mediums, okay?" She turned to Josh. "You're staying, right?"

Josh inspected his soggy socks, then nodded. "If you don't mind."

"Of course we don't mind," said Alison.

"We d–don't mind," called Benjie. Alison smiled. Benjie was wary of the world, men in particular; he'd stuttered like crazy when Marc used to come

around. Josh didn't scare the kid, though. Alison
didn't think Josh would scare anybody.

She closed her bedroom door and then put her
arms around Josh's neck. "I'm glad to see you," she
said softly, standing on tiptoes to brush his lips with
a butterfly kiss. She was glad. Before Josh rang the
doorbell, she'd been sitting alone at her desk,
making a chain of paper clips and thinking about
that afternoon, and Jeanette and Sheri and
Caroline. What would happen to Caroline and the
baby she was carrying inside her? Her friend's
predicament was haunting Alison; she couldn't
imagine what it was doing to Caro.

Josh freed his arms from the blanket and held
Alison close. They just stood like that until Alison
began to feel the damp from Josh's clothes through
her cotton jersey dress. "Don't think I'm being
forward or anything, but maybe you should get out
of that wet stuff. Let me throw it in the dryer."

When she returned from the laundry room in the
basement of the apartment building a few minutes
later, Josh was sitting on her bed modestly bundled
up to his neck in blankets. "Woofer says the pizza's
coming in half an hour," said Alison. "Your clothes
should be dry by then, too."

"Thanks. Just what you need, huh? Another kid
to take care of."

Alison climbed onto the bed beside him, settling
into the crook of his arm. "I don't mind. You know
you're always welcome over here. Seriously. Even
if my mother's home!" Mrs. Laurel hadn't approved
of Marc, but like Woofer and Benjie she seemed to
have more faith in Josh. Alison tipped her head to

look up at him. "But why aren't you eating dinner at home? Did Jason leave early or something?"

"No." Josh's eyes skittered away from hers. "He's still around."

"Oh." Alison had gotten the distinct feeling that Jason's visit hadn't lived up to Josh's expectations, but he'd been reticent about it. Even though they were closer than ever lately, she still knew better than to pry. With Josh it was always a delicate balance. The right touch opened him up like a flower in the sun; the wrong one and he hit the highway running.

So she didn't use words. Lifting one hand, she brushed his cheek with the backs of her fingers. Josh took her hand and turned it, kissing the palm. Then he rolled slightly away from her with a heavy sigh.

"It's rough," Alison began tentatively when Josh didn't speak. "It's rough when you need something from someone and they don't give it to you. It's happened to me. What I had to find out—the hard way—was that I wanted something that person couldn't ever have given me."

"But he's my brother," Josh said hoarsely. "If not him, who?"

Alison rubbed his shoulders. "You. Maybe you already have what it is that you need inside you, and you just don't know it."

Josh twisted so that he was facing her again. Alison was startled by the urgency in his eyes. They burrowed into her, taking shelter. "I have you, don't I?" he asked, his voice almost inaudible.

Her answer was a kiss. She meant it to be a brief one, but Josh deepened the kiss and wouldn't let

go. For an instant, Alison was surprised. She and
Josh had kissed and cuddled a number of times
since their first kiss opening night of *West Side
Story*, but they'd never crossed the line that separated affection from passion. She was pretty sure he
was a virgin, and for herself, she wanted to go
slowly. With Marc, things had gone so far so fast,
her body had left her heart and soul behind. She
wasn't going to let that happen again.

Josh's tongue tickled the roof of her mouth and
Alison felt herself growing warm. His body was
hard against hers; she slipped her arms beneath the
blanket and ran her hands down the warm, bare
skin of his back.

Then all at once her eyes filled with tears. They
spilled over, wetting Josh's face as well as her own.
He drew back, his expression alarmed and contrite
and embarrassed all at the same time.

"Alison, I'm sorry," he whispered. "I didn't plan
to come over here and act like an animal. I'm sorry.
Maybe you should go get my clothes out of the
dryer."

Alison had pulled her arms in and folded herself
up, but she hadn't withdrawn completely. "In a
minute," she said, hiding her face against Josh's
chest. "I'm the one that's sorry. I don't know why
I'm crying!"

"You don't need a reason. You don't have to
explain."

They lay quietly, just breathing. Alison kept her
eyes closed, and gradually she began to feel safe
again.

But maybe you were never really safe. Josh's
heart murmured a seashell sound in Alison's left

ear. *Caro's pregnant, and it could've been me*. It could have been her, with Marc. They'd made love, but Marc hadn't really loved' her. She would have been stranded emotionally, the same way Caro was. *Why does intimacy have to be so complicated?* Alison wondered sadly.

The doorbell rang. "Pizza man," guessed Josh, patting her gently on the head.

Alison sat up with a smile. Josh wasn't Marc, and she wasn't Caroline. The two of them had a lot to learn about each other, but so far they weren't doing so badly by taking it one step at a time.

THIRTEEN

"He's airborne. He slams it for two more points on the scoreboard. He's blowing away the competition."

Josh grabbed the basketball, amazed as usual that T.J. could shoot at all, seeing as how he spent so much energy yakking. He loped under the basket, his right arm arcing. *Swish*. "Ha!" Josh shouted. "Gotcha. We're tied, man."

"Not for long." T.J. backpedalled to the foul line he'd chalked on his family's blacktop driveway. Then he backpedalled some more, going for a three-pointer. He missed by about a mile, the basketball thunking against the backboard.

Josh grabbed the rebound, then made an easy shot from the foul line. "Guess you didn't play much hoops in California, huh?"

"Nope," T.J. confessed. "Volleyball was the sport of choice. Skateboarding. Frisbee." Swiping the ball from Josh, he did some fancy dribbling. "I remember seeing the Harlem Globetrotters on

T.V. when I was a kid, though. I could be one, what d'you think?"

Josh snorted. T.J. dribbled the ball between his legs, tripping over his own feet in the process.

Behind them, the early winter sun was dropping, its weak rays diluted by the spidery branches of a leafless tree. Josh rubbed his hands together, then blew on them. They were red and raw with the cold, but he went on playing one-on-one with T.J. Maybe if he hung around long enough, T.J. would ask him to stay for dinner. That way, he could put off going home a little longer.

T.J. the mind reader struck again. "Hey, Hickham, how come you're not messing around with your bro the superhero, anyway? He's still around, isn't he?"

Josh aimed the basketball, made a sloppy shot. Might as well tell T.J. the truth. For almost a week, since Thanksgiving, he'd been avoiding the house almost as much as he did before he ran away. That way he didn't have to face the fact that Jason was avoiding the house, too. "Yeah, he's still in town. He ships out again tomorrow."

"So, what are you doing wasting time with a buttface like me?"

"Dunno." Josh dribbled aimlessly for a moment. Then he passed the ball back to T.J., his hands too numb to shoot. It would probably sound petty and infantile. Josh made a halfhearted stab at explaining anyway. "I guess . . . I dunno. He's got other things to do. We just don't have all that much to talk about."

T.J. didn't act surprised, and he didn't start with the nosy questions. His attention seemed to be on the basketball, but Josh knew he was still listening. So he kept talking, as much to himself as to T.J.

"I thought it was gonna be different, that's all." Standing in the driveway, the wind slicing through him like a meat cleaver, Josh suddenly got that lost-at-sea feeling he'd had so often since his brother first left home for the Navy. "I mean, Jason always had his act together. I could depend on him. He never let me down." Josh thought for a moment, then added, "He never *meant* to let me down."

"And now?"

Josh blew on his hands some more. "He's just got other stuff on his mind. He doesn't have time for me."

T.J. must have been mulling this over as he set up for a lay-up, because right after the shot he made some kind of remark Josh only part heard—the wind ate half of it. "You gotta have realistic expectations," Josh thought T.J. said. And something about "standing on your own feet."

"You don't know what it's like," Josh retorted. T.J. stopped in mid-shot. He faced Josh, the basketball cradled in his arms. "You've got cool parents who you can talk to. I don't have anybody." Josh swallowed; his throat felt thick. "Jason's the only one in my joke of a family I was ever able to lean on."

"I didn't mean—"

"Aw, forget it." Josh waved a hand. "I gotta go—I'm frozen. Thanks for the game."

T.J. didn't try to stop him, just walked him to his bike. Josh gave him a feeble grin to let him know he wasn't mad; T.J. returned it.

The ride home was against the wind. Josh pedalled slowly, his whole body tensed against the cold. No place to go . . . the same old deal. Well, he could stop at the house, fortify himself with some chow, and brave the arctic wasteland of Split River Station. If he sat about one inch from the space heater, maybe he could get some sketching done.

The garage door was up and the car was gone. Somebody's out, Josh deduced. Could be the Witch, or Jason.

It was the Witch. Jason was camped in front of the T.V., with a half-brat on either side of him. Josh had to give his brother credit. The kids loved him for some reason—he'd completely won their pebble-sized hearts.

Jason had heard the door slam. "Hey, Jughead," he called over the tube's blare. "What's the news?"

"Nothin'." Josh clomped down the hall toward the kitchen, not slowing his pace or shifting his straight-ahead gaze.

He had his head in the fridge when Jason made him jump by yelling right behind him. "Okay, Jughead. Talk."

Josh threw a package of sliced ham and some cheese on the counter and began ransacking the cupboards for the bread. "What?"

The loaf of bread went sailing as Jason grabbed him in a body lock. "What's this, I gotta beat you up to get you to talk to me?"

Talk to you? That's all I've wanted to do for two weeks. Josh shook Jason off. Trying to act casual, he set about making a fat sandwich. "There, I'm talking. What d'you want me to say?"

Jason shoved aside a couple of their stepmother's cookbooks and hitched himself onto the counter. He wasn't messing around now; his expression had grown serious. "Just tell me why you're blowing me off and giving me the silent treatment."

"You blew me off first," Josh blurted out, slapping a piece of bread on top of the ham and cheese. "You're the one that, like, totally opted out of being a brother."

"In what way?"

"This vacation." Josh's voice failed him; the words came out cracked. "When Dad got sick. Every day for the past two years."

"Oh." Jason's blue eyes glinted with comprehension. "I let you down, huh?"

Throwing the cold cuts back in the fridge and trying not to do something totally embarrassing like cry, Josh nodded.

"I'm sorry, man," Jason said.

"Yeah, well." Josh bit into the sandwich.

Jason thought for a minute, kicking his feet rhythmically against the bottom cupboards. "I'm sorry about all of it," he continued. "I know it's been tough for you, living here. I wish I'd been around when Dad had the stroke. I wish I could've helped."

"Well, you weren't, were you? You didn't help. I got blamed." His eyes on the paper towel he was using for a plate, Josh chewed mechanically, even though the ham and cheese tasted bitter.

"What do you want to hear, Jughead? I'm guilty as charged. I'm a rotten brother and a rotten son."

Josh stared at Jason. For the first time, he saw

his brother stripped bare, a kid not much older than himself.

"This is the thing." Jason's tone turned intense. "I'd do anything to make it up to you, Jughead. Anything but tell you, 'Hell, go ahead, sign up for the Service like I did.' I won't sell you on the Navy."

"So, what else do I do?"

"You do what you want to do. You don't make the same mistake I did."

"But I don't know what I want. I'm not good at any damn thing."

Josh hated the self-pitying whine in his voice; he thought for sure his brother would hate it, too. Jason didn't gag, though. He just looked at Josh with this kind of sad, fond look. *He loves me*, Josh realized. All at once he felt warm. Jason wasn't infallible. He wasn't a god; he wasn't even much of a role model. But he was still his brother.

"Don't give me that crap," Jason ordered. "Think about it, man. Make up your own mind. You can't let me, or Dad, do it for you. If you do, you'll regret it the rest of your life."

"You regret it?"

Jason shrugged. "I told you what I think about the Navy nowadays. When I get out, I'll be starting over." He laughed, almost like he was embarrassed. "You probably won't believe this, but I kinda envy you. You could do it differently."

"I don't know about that."

"Yeah, you do. You've just gotta trust yourself that you know. It's in there."

Color, line, form. "I'm taking this life drawing

class at school. . . ." Josh couldn't believe he'd
said it.

"No kidding!" Jason exclaimed. "Man, that's what
I'm talking about. You've got talent."

"Mr. O'Dell thought so," Josh admitted. "He
talked me into taking the course."

"So, maybe this art teacher guy is the kind of
person you should be looking to for advice." Jason
slid off the counter. He socked Josh in the arm. "I'll
try to be around more for you. But the bottom line
is, you don't need me. You can make it on your
own."

Now Jason took a turn scrounging in the fridge.
When he reemerged with a can of beer and a
couple of apples, Josh had to restrain himself from
hugging him like a total mush.

Instead, he returned the punch in the arm.
Together, grub in hand, they headed back to the
living room to boot the half-brats off the couch.

Without Josh for a distraction, T.J. could let out all
the stops. He beat on the basketball, pounding it on
the pavement, hurling it at the backboard. His
hands were eggplant-purple from the cold and
scraped to hell from the goosebump surface of the
ball, but he kept on shooting. He made himself
sweat; he made himself hurt.

Nuts, that's what Caro'd say if she could see him.
Maybe he was. The self-flagellation was helping,
though. Purifying him, helping him see clearer.

Dunk. *I did the right thing, proposing.* Deep
down he was fairly sure of it. He'd been having his
doubts since Thanksgiving, though. Sure loving

Caroline, knowing she loved him back, had him floating on air. But the fact of her pregnancy was pretty effective at keeping his feet on the ground.

Dunk. *I must be out of my mind.* Get married, at the age of seventeen? To Caroline Buchanan, a girl he'd known for all of three months? If "known" was the right word, seeing as how she was the most elusive, enigmatic person he'd ever met.

Dunk. *I did the right thing.* But maybe his motives were screwy. Caroline was cornered. Was he taking advantage of her? Getting her any way he could? *"Be careful what you wish for because you might get it," that's how the saying goes. . . .*

"Hey, Magic!"

T.J. pivoted. Calamano was leaning out the open window of his dad's pick-up. "Shoot some hoops?" T.J. invited.

Marc parked at the curb and joined T.J. in the driveway. T.J. passed the ball; Marc's leather varsity jacket creaked as he made the shot.

"Can't believe I'm seeing you during daylight hours," observed T.J.

Marc grunted. "Team didn't make the county play-offs so the season's over. Gotta admit, I'm kind of at a loose end."

"Routine," T.J. agreed. "Even when you hate it, it's something to lean on."

"Yeah." Marc had possession; he dribbled idly. T.J. let him. Nobody took a ball from Calamano unless Calamano let him.

T.J. wondered if, now that he had time on his hands, Marc missed Alison. Not that half a dozen other girls weren't ready to hop into bed with him at any given moment. Sometimes, though, even for

a take-it-on-the-run guy like Marc, that kind of
thing had to be a little empty.

Suddenly T.J. had the urge to laugh out loud. He
was thinking about how Calamano would respond if
he told him about this marrying Caro idea. "So, just
pay for the abortion," Marc would say. "What, you
mean you haven't even *slept* with her? You're
gonna pay with the rest of your life for a lay you
didn't even get? I don't know, man. Sounds
dumb. . . ."

"So, what's on the calendar now football's over?"

Marc took a foul shot and passed the rebound to
T.J. "Football ain't over," Marc corrected him. "At
least, not at my house. Still got college and pro ball
blasting on the T.V. just about every night of the
week." T.J. missed his shot and Marc caught the
rebound. "Me, I'll probably wrestle. The coach is
always after me. I could kill 'em in heavyweight."
He missed a lay-up. "No hoops, that's for sure."

The sun had lost itself in a rim of red and purple
clouds at the horizon. An invisible agency turned
on the post light at the bottom of the driveway,
enabling T.J. and Marc to see. *Mom*, T.J. thought.

"Thought I'd catch you cramming," said Marc.

"Huh?"

"The city scholarship test thing, Bonehead. It's
tomorrow, right?"

"Yeah." In the process of abusing his body, T.J.
had almost forgotten about the test. Should he even
bother taking it? What was the point? He wasn't
going to college next year. He'd be working at some
low-level job, coming home to a wife and kid. "I'm
in pretty good shape for it. Just giving my brain a
good night's rest."

"Break a leg, man."

"Thanks."

"I bet you win it."

"I've already dusted a spot on the shelf for the trophy," T.J. assured him. Suddenly, though, he felt boneless and feeble. The exertion was catching up with him. His biceps burned; his knuckles were stiff. *Probably won't be able to lift a pencil tomorrow.*

What made him think he was strong enough to take care of himself and her both, plus a baby? "You're nuts," Caro had said when he presented the idea last Thursday. Maybe she was right.

"Mom, what's the story?" asked T.J. If anything, there was more food on the table than at Thanksgiving, and his mother didn't usually cook on weeknights. "The three of us are supposed to eat all this?"

Mrs. McAllister distributed plates. "I'll admit, I went overboard. It's a good luck feast, that's all. I got home early from school and decided I'd make your favorite food. So I started thinking mashed potatoes, broccoli au gratin, spare ribs and next thing I knew, I had about ten things going on in the oven and on top of the stove."

"You're going to make me feel guilty if I don't win," T.J. said, filling his glass from the skim milk carton.

"That's what mothers are for. I'm just not going to feed you ever again if you don't get the scholarship. Only kidding, sweetie."

"Yeah, I bet." T.J. gnawed on a spare rib. A good

luck feast, for God's sake. But of course she didn't know. She was just kidding around about the guilt stuff. She didn't know.

"Do you feel like you're ready for the test?" his father asked.

"You bet," T.J. declared. "I've read all the books twice and my skull is bursting with brilliance. The scholarship committee will be on their knees bowing to the incisive originality of my essays."

"You always did test well," Mrs. McAllister commented.

"You know, we're proud of you," added Mr. McAllister, "for trying for this thing."

T.J. made a pool for the butter in his mashed potatoes, avoiding his dad's gaze. "Yeah, well. I just want to do my part."

"With that scholarship, you could go to any school you wanted," his mother mused. "Harvard, Princeton, Yale."

"The world would be my oyster," T.J. said heartily.

"Not that the university here would be so bad," she continued. "We could manage the tuition easily—I'd get a break for you because I'm on the faculty. One way or another, you'll get your chance."

"I don't doubt it," T.J. said. Then he concentrated on shoving broccoli into his mouth. His mom had made all his favorite foods, and he'd already decided to forgo the scholarship even if he did win it. Here they sat, rapping about his future. The three of them had always been a team. They treated him like an equal; they treated him better than an equal, because they also treated him like a son.

"Cool parents you can talk to," Josh said. *How the hell am I ever going to tell them?*

"What about Caroline?" Mrs. McAllister was asking. "It sounded to me like she was having a harder time settling down with the books. Did she ever make it through the reading list?"

T.J. swallowed the broccoli. He wiped his mouth on his paper napkin. His whole body had gone numb; his brain was numb. Caroline and the reading list . . . "As a matter of fact, she dropped out of the contest. She's pregnant and she's going to have the baby and I'm going to help her. I'm skipping college."

Did I really say it? Through the fuzz that had suddenly carpeted his eyes, T.J. thought he saw his father's jaw harden, his mother's face twist with shock and disbelief.

Then his vision defuzzed. His parents were waiting for a response. Relief. "Caro? Actually, I don't think she did make it through the list. I think she's planning to wing it."

"I'm glad you at least have your feet on the ground," Mrs. McAllister said. "Here, you've got to try this. I don't know what I did, but it came out even better than usual."

T.J. helped himself dutifully. He'd keep on eating—he'd eat it all. But it was the Last Supper, sort of, and he was Judas. He couldn't put off telling them forever.

FOURTEEN

"Should have showed up half an hour ago," Caroline told T.J. as he kicked the snow off his shoes at the door of her apartment. "Suzi modelled her new snow-bunny outfit before she and my dad left for their Pocono Mountain ski weekend at the place with the heart-shaped beds and bathtubs."

"Let me guess. Candy pink."

Carol laughed. "Worse than candy pink. *Neon* candy pink. I guess so my dad won't lose her on the slopes when they ski at night."

"Talk about heart-shaped beds and bath-tubs. . . ." T.J. looked around the living room. There was a fire in the fireplace and cheese and fruit and a loaf of French bread on the coffee table. "Looks like you're ready for a little après ski romance yourself."

Caroline turned, swinging her long hair to hide her expression. She never blushed, but she was blushing now; the warmth of her face felt strange.

"I was just about to pig out. Eating for two, you know."

"Yeah. I know."

T.J. stuck his shoes and coat in the closet. Caro sat down cross-legged on the floor with her back against the couch and he sprawled out behind her, one arm extended and draped over her shoulder.

She took his hand in hers and played with his fingers, bending them one by one. "You never told me about the nerd-fest the other day. Did you score big?"

Caroline hadn't much wanted to ask this question. She knew T.J. had turned ambivalent about the scholarship contest recently, and she knew why.

Now, to her surprise, he actually got a little bit gung-ho about it. In a sincere way, too. He wasn't just trying to make her feel better. "You know, I got in there and I really got pumped. I don't know what it was." She turned her head and caught his grin. "The stimulating sound of pencils sharpening, the smell of sweat, those little blue exam booklets . . ."

"What a turn-on."

"Yeah, well, it does it for me every time. So, I don't know what came over me, but I pretty much gave it everything I got. I mean, I probably won't win the scholarship, and even if I do I probably won't take it." Caroline held her breath, but T.J. was just talking straight, without resentment. "It was fun. I knew more than I thought I did."

"Just as well I didn't go for it," Caro said, leaning forward to cut a wedge of brie. "I'm no good at being intellectual and objective."

"You react to characters in books like they're real people. That's valid."

"Yeah, but it doesn't exactly make for a proper response to essay test questions."

"Well, it's done and I'm psyched. No more living in the library like a candidate for class geek."

Caroline twisted to give him a chunk of bread and cheese. "Welcome back to the real world."

He held her eyes for a long moment. Then he changed the subject, but not really. "How're you feeling today?"

"Okay." Unconsciously, she rested her hands on her stomach as she answered. "I was having some more of those cramps earlier, but I'm fine now."

T.J. tightened his arm around her. "Have you talked to anybody at the clinic about that stuff? I don't know, it just doesn't sound quite right to me."

"And you're an obstetrician, right?"

"Sure." He grinned. "One of my many side-lines."

"I'm fine," she repeated. Then she laughed at herself. *Fine—right. Pregnant and just fine.*

T.J. must have heard the ironic note in her laugh. "Are you going to be able to manage it?" he asked, his eyes intent on her face. "Having the baby—being a mother?"

She'd never mentioned visiting Jeanette, how mixed-up that scene left her—half-exhilarated, half-terrified, and none too sure motherhood was a role she could adapt to. "I don't know," she said frankly. "I stopped in on a friend on Monday—a girl I used to hang around with when I went out with Brad Gradowski." She caught T.J.'s tightened jaw. "Who, by the way, is not—he's not the one. . . ."

T.J. put a finger over her lips. "It's okay. You don't have to. So what about this girlfriend?"

"She has a baby," Caro continued. "She's a year older than me. Same kind of thing."

"Is she married or doing it alone?"

"Married. They have a cute little house." Caroline laughed. "Listen to me—'cute little house.' Like I'm into the white picket fence scene. Anyway, she was really honest with me, about how sometimes it's wonderful and sometimes it sucks. I mean, it's hard. You have to make sacrifices."

"But if you're making sacrifices for something worthwhile . . ."

"For a child," Caroline said softly. "For love. Yeah, that's the way she talked. She said it was worth it. And I could see that. I could see how it was worth it, I could feel it. But T.J., it still scared me. I looked at her and she just looked so young. So young to be a mom. And you can't change your mind. Once you have the kid, it's yours for life." Her eyes narrowed. "Or it's supposed to be, anyway."

T.J. kissed her hair. Now Caro threw him a question of her own. "But what about you?" He couldn't fool her; she knew him too well to miss the recent signs of serious second thoughts. "What about *you?*"

T.J. pulled her up on the sofa next to him. He cupped her face in his hands. His green eyes, glinting in the firelight, gave her all the answer she needed. "If you"—he patted her stomach—"the two of you want me, the offer still stands."

Then Caroline knew. With this guy, this best friend who made her crazy with desire, she could do it. "I want you." She smiled. "In the worst way."

Sliding his hands down to her shoulders, T.J. kissed her. A long, sweet kiss—a pledge. After, he sat back on the couch looking sheepish. "I don't have a ring or anything. I'm kind of new at this getting engaged and having babies stuff."

"I don't want a ring," Caroline said with certainty, "and we don't even have to get married. We can just be . . . together."

"Sounds good to me." All of a sudden, a fireworks-caliber grin burst across T.J.'s thin face. He catapulted up from the couch, grabbed Caroline, and spun her around. "Man, we're gonna be parents! How d'you like that?"

She liked it. For the first time in weeks, Caroline forgot to be scared and uptight. For the first time, she felt joy.

"This calls for a celebration." T.J. raced for the kitchen and returned with a bottle of sparkling water and a couple glasses.

"Isn't there anything better in there? My dad almost always has champagne chilling. Suzi drinks it like it was soda."

T.J. shook a finger at her. "No hard stuff, Ms. Buchanan. Remember, you're eating *and* drinking for two."

Caroline pretended to be ticked, but she liked T.J. taking care of her. Most of the time, she didn't even take care of herself. Now she had a reason to.

Back on the couch, they assumed their favorite lounging position, halfway reclining with their legs in a comfortable tangle. T.J. raised his glass of sparkling water. "Here's to the wackiest couple since Bonnie and Clyde."

Caroline returned the toast. "No kidding. We'll probably be turning to armed robbery before we're through. How are we gonna pull this off?"

"Easy." T.J. crumbled her doubts like a stale cookie. "We get our diplomas from Nowhere High."

"God, *June*. I'll be a whale!"

"Enormous," T.J. agreed. "Then we blow this town. Say good-bye to our buddies and Split River Station, and split for Pittsburgh or Philly or wherever you want. You'll just keep getting bigger and I'll get employment."

"Doing what?"

His reply was prompt. "Computers. I'm on a fair way to being a whiz. I should be able to find something at an entry level."

He's got it all figured out, Caroline marvelled silently. She dropped her eyes and concentrated on tickling T.J.'s knee through a rip in his jeans. "But what about . . . college?"

His optimism didn't fade one watt. "It can wait a year or so. We've got the rest of our lives."

The rest of our lives . . . Caroline looked up at T.J. "I've never been good at sticking around," she began. "But I think I can stick with you." She teased him with a smile. "How 'bout you, though? You still gonna think I'm hot fifty years from now, when my boobs sag and I trade in the blue jeans for polyester pantsuits?"

"Hot isn't the word. You don't know what polyester does to me."

Caroline took his glass and put it and hers both on the coffee table. Then she turned back to T.J., stretching herself out on top of him. He wrapped

his arms around her, holding her body to his,
making them one body.

For a moment, before their lips met in a kiss,
Caroline caught a glimpse of the future. She'd go
back to the clinic and let them know she was having
the baby; they'd schedule her for regular checkups.
Then there were so many people to tell. . . .

Soon enough. Soon enough they'd have to deal
with the horror and hassle. Tonight, though, it was
just the two of them. Her and T.J., finally. Forever.

Caroline put her mouth on T.J.'s and they kissed
like they'd never kissed before, their special fierce
passion deepened by the promise of committed
love.

Caroline became breathless. She was impatient
to feel T.J.'s hands all over her, to touch him all
over. Meanwhile he held back for a moment. There
was a funny look in his eyes, like he was asking
permission. She smiled. "You've got a green light,
McAllister. If we're gonna live together and be
parents, we should probably find out if we're
really . . . *compatible*."

"Exactly what I was thinking."

It didn't even occur to Caroline that after all the
waiting for it and wanting it, the love-making itself
could be a disappointment. And it wasn't. As she
and T.J. came together, moved together, the pleasure was so sweet and fine it almost hurt. T.J. found
a place inside her that no one else had ever
reached.

Caroline drifted in and out of sleep, deliciously
drowsy and full of dreams. T.J. was totally out, his

arms heavy and warm around her, his breathing slow.

She savored the closeness. It was something altogether new, not her usual post-sex sensation. But then, she'd never had sex like what she just shared with T.J. It was more than just feeling good—it was beautiful. It meant more, that was all, so much more than the sex she'd had with Leon or Craig or any of the other guys, because T.J. was the first one she'd ever really loved.

In a way, Caro thought, with a feeling close to awe, *T.J. is the father of my baby. We just made it that way.* If this little heaven could only last forever.

Not a chance. The phone rang, jolting her out of her dreams. She almost let it go, then reached to grab the receiver. "Hello?" Her voice came out husky, and she almost giggled. She *sounded* like somebody cooling down after a hot one.

"Caro, that you? It's Darcy."

"Darce! What's going on?"

"Look out your window—it's snowing! It's been snowing for hours! Josh and Alison are over here, and Phil—"

"Phil?"

"Yeah." Caroline could picture her friend's characteristic blush. "From school," Darcy added unhelpfully.

"Oh, *that* Phil," Caro teased. "Gotcha."

Darcy laughed. "Well, we're going sledding in my yard. Pick up T.J. and come on over, okay?"

Caroline hung up the phone. T.J.'s eyelids were half open and about to drop again. She shook him. "Look alive, McAllister. I'm supposed to pick you up and escort you to the Jenner estate for some sledding."

"I'd rather you picked me up and . . ." T.J. suggested.

Caroline shook her head, pretending to be disgusted. "Once is just never enough, huh?"

When they got outside, they were both glad Darcy had called. The night was too rare for sleep—the fresh, new snow was still sifting down from the goosedown sky. For a moment, they just stood, listening to the whisper. Then Caroline grabbed T.J.'s hand and raced. She wanted to make the Mustang's engine roar.

At the car, though, she paused, then tossed the keys to T.J. "You get to drive tonight."

"This my reward," he kidded, "for services rendered?"

She nailed him with a fistful of fluffy snow. "Just don't aim for any more fences."

T.J. maintained a conservative thirty miles per hour the whole way to Darcy's, stalling out at three out of four stop signs, but otherwise appearing to have gotten the hang of it.

"King of the road," said Caroline as T.J. braked at the gates marking the Jenners' long driveway. She remembered T.J.'s driving lesson in the school parking lot a couple weeks ago, the secret she'd been harboring. What big steps she'd—they'd—taken since then.

They parked the Mustang under the Jenners's carport. The shouts of the others led Caro and T.J. around the big grey fieldstone house. Darcy, Phil, Alison, and Josh were gathered at the top of a hill sloping down to the edge of the woods. "Your folks must be away, too," Caroline guessed. "What are you sledding on, silver tea trays?"

Darcy threw a snowball. T.J. ducked it. "Flying saucers from K-Mart," she assured Caro. "My parents *are* away, but the maid's still here and I'd have to smuggle silver out of the house over her dead body."

"Hi, Caro!" A snow-covered Mouse threw her arms around Caroline while Josh tossed a snowball at T.J. This time T.J. took it in the nose.

Alison made it clear she thought it was a healthy sign for Caro to be out with her friends. *Wait till she hears the latest,* Caro thought, hiding her smile by bending over to scoop up a mittenful of snow. She'd have to tell Alison she'd decided to go through with the pregnancy. Mouse was going to be an aunt.

Somebody'd brought a thermos of hot chocolate. Phil, who Caroline recognized from the football team, poured some out and offered it to her. He was a little jockish and conservative, she judged, but a friendly guy. "Thanks," she said, holding the mug of hot chocolate to her face and warming her nose in its steam.

Meanwhile, Darcy was pulling Phil toward the edge of the hill. The two collapsed onto a flying saucer and spun off down the slope, screaming.

"Looks like fun," T.J. observed, dubious.

"Mmm."

Now it was Josh and Alison's turn. They settled onto their flying saucer with more style, Josh holding Alison on his lap. Then they sat there for a second, stuck in the snow, until T.J. gave them the necessary shove. Caroline pelted them with a snowball. "Bon voyage!"

The snow was tapering off. As Caroline handed the hot chocolate to T.J., she turned her eyes upward. Through the broken clouds, the brilliant stars looked close enough to touch. *Just grab a saucer and go*, she instructed herself. *Act like a kid like everybody else*.

She couldn't.

T.J. didn't seem to notice. He'd stuck the thermos back in the snow and was busy stockpiling snowballs to bombard the rest of the gang on their return.

Doesn't he realize? Caroline wondered sadly. A year from now Mouse and Darce and Phil and everybody would be back here, or somewhere, messing around like this. Snowball fights and sledding and laughing and yelling. Whereas she and T.J. . . .

T.J. broke into her thoughts. Once again he blew her doubts away like the winter wind. Abandoning the snowballs, he came up behind her and enveloped her in a snowy bear hug. "I'm ready for the ride of my life," he declared, pushing her toward the slope.

"Oh, McAllister, nooo . . . !"

She and T.J. were whirling down the hill in the dark. Caro's hair flew and the cold wind stole her breath. Holding onto T.J. with all her might, she shrieked with laughter.

Before they reached the bottom of the hill, Caroline had time to discover something. Taking on adult responsibilities didn't have to mean giving up all the fun. She had a feeling that with T.J., life would always be an adventure.

Crash. Almost at the foot of the slope, their

flying saucer hit a bump and sent Caro and T.J. sailing. They landed in a tangle of arms and legs.

T.J. was helpless, laughing. Caro would have been laughing, but she'd had the breath knocked out of her. For a few seconds, she could only gasp, bending over and clutching her waist. T.J.'s grin dissolved. He brushed the snow from her face and hair and rubbed her shoulders, his forehead creased with anxiety. "Are you all right?"

Caroline finally sucked down some air. She could laugh again, and she did. She shoved T.J. away and scrambled to her feet. "You old mother hen, McAllister."

T.J. gripped the flying saucer under one arm and put the other arm around Caroline's shoulders. Together they started back up the hill to join their friends.

FIFTEEN

"T.J. . . . T.J. . . . ."

He swam upwards from the sea-depths of sleep, his arms flailing into something soft. *Caro*, his fogged brain remembered happily.

She was sitting up in bed, her knees hunched. In the dark, T.J. couldn't read her face, but as she repeated his name, he could hear her distress. "T.J., wake up."

"I'm here," he assured her, sitting up, too.

"I don't feel well."

The little-girl complaint, the quiver in Caroline's voice—in anybody else it might not mean much. T.J. knew Caro too well, though. He caught her fear like a virus. "What's wrong?"

"Cramps."

She was bending forward, hugging her knees. When T.J. put a hand to her face to brush aside the hair, he felt the damp of tears. "Bad?"

"Worse than the others I've had."

It was the dead of night, and black. Three-thirty,

T.J. saw by the clock radio. Only a couple hours since they returned from Darcy's, made love again, tenderly, and hit the sack.

"I just woke up," Caroline was saying. "At first, it hurt so much I thought I was still in a dream. Then I realized I wasn't."

T.J. put a hand out to the lamp next to Caro's bed, then squinted as the yellow light split open the dark of the bedroom. Caroline had the sheet pulled up to her chin; her hair was tangled and her eyes were wide. He reached for her, but she hunched her shoulders away from his touch. "I think . . . I think I need to go to the bathroom."

Red. He saw it on the sheet the same moment she did. "Oh, my God," she whispered, hoarse with terror. "I'm bleeding."

It was like a nightmare. Maybe she *was* dreaming, and him, too, T.J. thought. Something had gone wrong.

Sitting on the edge of the bed, Caroline froze, unable to act. It was T.J. who decided what to do. He wrapped her in a bathrobe and a blanket, then carried her downstairs in his arms like she was a child. Outside, the fresh snow was smooth under the stars, but he ran through it without seeing it, his eyes on the Mustang and his mind on the question of how many minutes it would take to get to the hospital. His stupid learner's permit, and the driving practice with Caroline—he thanked God for it now. He just had to stay calm. *Clutch up, gas down*. . . .

"You're going to be okay," he promised Caroline. Her arms tightened around his neck; she buried her face against his chest. "You're going to be okay."

* * *

"They said I don't need to be admitted," Caroline told T.J., her voice flat and colorless. "I'm pretty weak, but the bleeding's stopped. When we get home, I'm supposed to spend the rest of the day in bed, that's all."

T.J.'s eyes had a buggy look, from the glare and tension of the emergency room waiting area, Caroline supposed. He stared down at her as if he hadn't understood her words. She felt naked wearing that hospital gown, and exposed. The collapsible bed-thing she was lying on was only separated from the rest of the emergency room by a flimsy curtain. Naked and exposed—and empty.

Her eyes moved to the blood-stained bathrobe, balled up on a chair next to her bed. *It was just blood. That's really all it was—just a shapeless little clot of blood. It wasn't really a baby yet.*

She wasn't even sure if T.J. knew. No, he had to. He'd have been asking everybody what was going on, like any anxious friend-husband-father type. *Not a father anymore, though.* Someone probably told him: "Not much we can do. She's already miscarried."

Caroline had been avoiding T.J.'s eyes. Now she looked straight at him. He was crying. "God, T.J. Don't."

"I just feel like . . . it was my fault," he said, anguished. "I didn't take care of you. We shouldn't have gone sledding at Darcy's last night." He flushed and she saw his jaw clench. "We shouldn't have made love. I shouldn't have touched you."

"I really don't think—" Caroline broke off as the

OB/GYN intern who'd examined her stepped up to her bed.

The intern handed Caro a yellow slip. "A prescription for a pain reliever," he explained. "In case you have any more cramping. Aspirin's no good in a situation like this. It thins blood—you need the clotting."

The intern's eyes shifted to T.J.'s distraught face and then back to Caroline's. "Sorry to eavesdrop, kids, but let's clear up something here. Sledding and sex are fine activities for women at almost any stage of pregnancy. They don't cause miscarriages. Most likely there was something wrong with the fetus from the start. The cramps you were having all along, Caroline, indicated a problem. Miscarriages in the first trimester are by no means uncommon, especially for teenagers." He squeezed Caroline's shoulder. "You'll get another chance. Need anything else?"

She shook her head. A relieved T.J. looked about ready to kiss the hem of the intern's scrubs. "No. Thanks."

They were alone again.

"Tell you what—I'll take the car back to your place and get you some clothes, okay?" T.J. suggested.

Caroline could tell he was dying to feel helpful and practical. She nodded.

"I'll be back in five." T.J. hesitated, hovering over her. Then he bent down to kiss her. She turned her face away; his lips just brushed her cheek. She stayed facing the wall until she heard him leave.

Physically, Caroline felt a little better forty-five

minutes later when she put on the jeans and
sweater T.J. brought with him. "I'm still me," she
said, forcing a dry laugh.

"Are you sure you're all right to go home?" he
asked.

"They're kicking me out. They need this bed in
case some *real* sick people come in." Still, she
wobbled a little as she walked along the corridor,
even with T.J. supporting her.

The Mustang, the smell of it and the feel of it,
infused Caroline with a soothing shot of security.
She sat down, stiff and ginger, then she relaxed.
She was back in her cocoon, she was okay.

It was a bright early December morning; the sun
bounced off the snow, which was melting fast.
Caroline closed her eyes against the light. *Not
okay.* It hurt. *She* hurt.

T.J. didn't try to make conversation. He fiddled
with the radio volume, getting it just right, then did
the same with the heat. He drove Caroline
smoothly home, as if he'd been doing it all his
life—didn't stall once. After parking in front of her
apartment building, he hurried around to her side
of the car. They stepped up to the sidewalk, T.J.
gripping her arm. Caroline shook him off. "You
make me feel like an old lady."

He smiled awkwardly. For once, she had him off
balance. For once, he didn't know how to act.
Under any other circumstances, Caro would have
considered it a victory. She hadn't won anything,
though; she'd lost.

She wouldn't let herself think about it. *Numb. I
just want to be numb.*

T.J. made Caroline sit on the couch while he

stripped the sheets from her bed and made it up with clean ones. Then he left her alone to undress. When he reappeared in her bedroom, he was carrying a tray with graham crackers and steaming tea.

He set the tray on the night table and sat on the edge of her bed. He was smiling, like he'd decided that being cheerful was the right way to approach her. "Always wanted to be a candy striper," he said, holding the cup of tea to her lips and then handing her a graham cracker.

She didn't smile; she didn't frown. She just took the graham cracker and held it. It was brown, with those little holes, and a dusting of cinnamon. All of a sudden, looking at it, Caroline felt like a kid again. Sick in bed with her mom fussing over her, feeling her forehead for fever, giving her ginger ale and graham crackers. A kid and a mother. *My mom*. *Me*.

The sobs started slowly, they came from so deep inside her. She pressed her hands to her face, but nothing was going to stop the tears. She'd lost. Again.

She couldn't see him because of the tears, but she felt him as he put his arms around her and held her close. His hand stroked her hair, he whispered over and over, "Sshh. Sshh. I've got you. I'm here."

It took a while, but finally the choking sobs subsided. Caroline caught her breath and laughed through her tears. "Sorry. I don't know what came over me."

"No, I'm sorry." T.J.'s arms tightened around her. "I'm so sorry, Caro," he whispered.

"But we shouldn't be." She wiped her nose

against the sleeve of T.J.'s shirt. She hadn't been *very* pregnant. She didn't even want to be pregnant in the first place. So if anything, she should be happy. "I don't understand myself."

T.J. fumbled for an explanation, the breath of his words warm against her neck. "The shock—you should try to sleep—"

The tears started again and Caro held onto T.J. for her life. Maybe she hadn't planned to become pregnant, but she'd ended up accepting it, and almost looking forward to the life she and T.J. and the baby were going to build together. She loved T.J., and she would have worked hard at loving her baby. Now she was alone again, just one solitary, hollow person. If only she'd never discovered what it was like to be different. *I won't cry. I won't feel sorry for myself.* She could take care of herself. She always had.

Caroline pushed T.J. away from her. She sat up, sniffling, and reached for a graham cracker. T.J. was looking at her, and as he looked at her, she could feel it happen. She felt her eyes dry and the emotion smooth out of her face. But even as she started to close the emotional door, she paused. She didn't want to go back in the old shell. *Call me back, T.J.*

"Nothing's changed."

"What?" said Caroline, startled.

"I mean, because of this. Nothing else has changed."

She brushed some crumbs off the front of her night shirt, composed. "Everything's changed."

"It doesn't change how much I love you," he said quietly.

Her mouth twisted, a bitter-sad smile. "You still think we're going to live happily ever after?"

He grinned. "I'll let you off the hook about 'ever after' for now. What I want, all I ever wanted, is for you to be part of my life."

She remembered it all then, all they'd struggled with and talked about and planned during the last couple weeks. The steps they'd taken together. "You don't have to bail me out anymore, McAllister. The heat's off."

"No, it's not."

She knew what he meant. It wasn't. The pressure from her being pregnant was gone, but the main reason for the whole crazy getting married plan was still there. Now she had to say it. When she'd said it before, it was for the baby, too. She had to say it for herself.

Caroline put out a hand. Tentatively, she brushed the floppy long hair back from T.J.'s forehead. "Aw, McAllister. I love you."

It wasn't a question; it didn't require an answer. Caro felt T.J.'s love. It was all around her. It had been, ever since they first became friends.

SIXTEEN

T.J. hooted as Marc presented himself at the door of Split River Station shouldering a small pine tree. "Pull that up by the roots, big guy?"

Marc propped the tree against the far wall. "It's a good one, if I do say so myself."

"A Christmas tree extraordinaire," agreed T.J. "Whose yard did you sabotage?"

"Hey, I'm no trespasser." Marc grinned. "Well, it was just the *back* yard."

By stacking some loose bricks around the base of the trunk, they got the tree in a stable upright position. Marc stepped back to admire it. Then he frowned. "We don't do this sort of thing at my house, but it seems to me like, I don't know—it's missing something."

"Decorations," said T.J. "I'll show you decorating." He ripped a page of comics off the wall, one with a nice big picture of Superman. Tearing carefully, he liberated Superman, then stuck him on the top branch of the tree.

"I thought, like, a star or an angel was supposed to go on top."

"Anything goes at Split River Station," T.J. reminded him.

"That's right." Marc laughed dryly. "The famous 'no-rules' rule."

"Exactly."

Marc hit the couch, T.J. took a lawn chair; both of them faced the space heater. Marc had brought a six-pack and he prepared to toss a can. T.J. waved it off. "It's the holiday season." He reached into his backpack. "Gotta drink this stuff."

"Eggnog? No way, man. I *hate* that stuff."

T.J. opened the carton and raised it for a gulp. He licked his lips. "Umm, good."

Marc snapped the top on a beer. "Gag me. By the way, tough luck about the scholarship contest."

"Yeah." T.J. shrugged. It was over. They'd named the winner and it wasn't him. He'd been ready for it, though. He wasn't exactly at his best the day of the exam; it'd be the understatement of the century to say he'd been distracted.

"I'll get there somehow," T.J. said, meaning college. *Weird*, he thought to himself. How fast, since Caro's miscarriage, he'd fallen back into the old way of viewing the future. High school, college, a job—in that order. *Then* marriage and a family. "Don't suppose you got a scholarship to spare?"

"Sure, if you want to slap the pigskin around for some podunk state U."

T.J. considered it. "I get a feeling somebody would scent the substitution." He chugged some more eggnog instead of asking the natural question. He didn't know whether Marc planned to sell out and take a football scholarship, or if he was finally going to break out of the mold his family and a succession of coaches had forced him into.

Marc balanced the can on the back of the sofa. "It's only December. I'm not gonna worry about any of that stuff till April or May."

T.J. nodded. What was the rush, anyway? For him, in the few days since Caroline woke him up in the middle of the night, the future had receded. They'd all get there soon enough.

"Yo, anybody home?" The recalcitrant station door bucked open; in fell Darcy, followed by Caro. "Oh, a tree!" Darcy exclaimed. "Wish I'd known. We have boxes and boxes of beautiful antique ornaments at my house—" She caught herself with a smile. "Then again, we could just string some popcorn."

T.J. heard Darcy but his eyes were on Caroline, for a change. There was snow on her fine brown hair and her cheeks and nose were red from the cold. T.J. thought she looked more beautiful than he'd ever seen her, but then he thought that every damn time he looked at her.

When she smiled at him, he saw the something softer, sadder, older that had stolen behind her eyes lately. An instant later, though, she was the old Caroline—laughing at the Superman Christmas tree and the eggnog, sitting down hard on his lap on purpose in order to try and tip over the lawn chair.

Darcy put a cassette in the tape player. Caro groaned when she heard it. "Bruce Springsteen singing 'Santa Claus Is Coming to Town'—talk about a foolproof way to destroy a Christmas carol."

"It's either that or this." Darcy held up another

tape. "Bing Crosby singing stuff like 'Chestnuts Roasting.'"

"We could sing our own carols," T. J. suggested. He cleared his throat, preparatory to belting out his personal favorite, "We Three Kings." Caroline shut him up with a kiss.

"You know what this place needs?" Darcy munched one of the Christmas cookies she and Caroline had brought. "It needs—"

"Josh and Mouse!" declared Caroline, as the door to the station flew open and there they were.

"Well, sure," Darcy conceded. "But I was going to say lights."

"We got lights." Alison pulled a string of them out of the grocery bag in Josh's arms. "The little twinkly colored ones that look like rainbow stars."

Could be an iota of tension, T. J. anticipated, sensitive to the lingering Marc-Alison-Josh triangle effect. Come to think of it, Caro and Marc rubbed each other wrong sometimes, and for all he knew there was a loose end or two between Darcy and Josh. All the pieces of the puzzle of life; even when you got them together, they never fit exactly perfect. Then again, T. J. supposed, it wouldn't be any fun if they did.

Might as well do what he could to ease everybody into their places. "Hand 'em over," he ordered, pushing Caro off his lap so he could take the bag of lights from Josh. "Hey, Calamano. Give me a hand with these."

Marc and T. J. got busy stringing lights around the station. There were three strands, and as T. J. went to plug the last one into the battery that ran the space heater, he saw Mouse pat Caro's shoulder—a small secret gesture, containing a world of support and sympathy. Darcy and Josh, meanwhile, were debating the mood-music issue. Bing finally won, and the corny, crackly strains of "White Christmas" filled the station just as the colored lights flashed on.

They all oohed and ahhed over the effect like it was the lighting of the Christmas tree in Rockefeller Center or something. "Not bad," T.J. acknowledged.

"Not bad? You scrooge," Caroline accused him. "It looks great. C'mon, let's make some more ornaments."

She started pulling comic book pages off the wall and T.J. joined her. "Hey, be careful," T.J. cautioned. "Lois has a lot of nice curves. Don't miss any of 'em."

Caro laughed. "Don't you tear anything essential off ol' Superman, either."

"Or he'll start talking like this," T.J. squeaked in a falsetto.

He didn't notice until they were done; they'd stripped off most of the Superman wallpaper. The bare space on the wall gave T.J. a funny feeling. *We'll be moving on*, he realized suddenly. Maybe in a way they'd outgrown the station already.

Thud. "What was that?" asked Caro.

"Something against the window," said T.J. "Didn't sound like a rock, though."

"A snowball maybe." Marc strode to the door. "Yo!" he bellowed out into the night. "Hey, I see you runts!"

T.J. and Caro joined him. Among the rustling stalks of dead weeds, T.J. could see three or four shadowy forms dodging. Just kids, and scrawny looking ones at that. A few more snowballs pelted towards the station.

"It's a raid!" T.J. shouted, bending to scoop up some snow. "This is a warning, we take no prisoners!"

He heard laughter on the cold wind, then the kids disappeared into the night. T.J. guessed they'd glimpsed Calamano, the giant, and figured they didn't stand much of a chance of taking over the fort.

"Shut the door," Darcy called. "It's already an ice box in here!"

Caroline and T.J. settled back down pretzel-style on the lawn chair. Darcy and Marc occupied the couch; Josh and Alison, paintbrushes in hand, were at the wall adding to Josh's mural. Bing was crooning "Oh, Come all Ye Faithful."

"So, Darce." Marc took the ends of Darcy's long wool scarf and tugged her towards him. "Do I get credit for matchmaking or what?"

Darcy pushed him off, laughing. The Darcy blush struck; her cheeks turned carnation pink. "Am I supposed to believe you had an ulterior motive that day you dragged me to the jock lunch table?"

"I dragged her," Marc said to T.J. and Caroline. "By the hair."

"I bet," T.J. remarked.

"Yeah, I heard that story," said Caro. "Sounded like real punishment to me, having to eat lunch with a tableful of muscle-bound hunks."

Darcy tossed a throw pillow at her.

"Just wondering, 'cause Phil's keeping pretty

closed about you," said Marc. "Despite being hounded for details in the locker room."

"Wow, a jock with integrity," Caro commented dryly.

He just grinned, not bothering to respond in kind to Caro's sarcasm. *Marc must be in a mellow mood*, T.J. surmised.

"You'll just have to look for the story on the society page," Darcy told Marc coyly.

T.J. glanced over at Josh and Mouse. One of them had painted a sprig of mistletoe on the wall; they stood beneath it, kissing. "Hey, none of that!" T.J. shouted.

Marc looked their way, too, then dropped his eyes, acting intent on playing with the fringe of Darcy's scarf.

T.J. wasted no time filling the sudden awkward silence. "Too bad we're the only ones who get to see Hickham's mural," he remarked. "If you ask me, it should stand side by side with the one in the main lobby at school."

"I kind of had that in mind while I painted this," Josh admitted, stepping back from it. "Everything about that one's so unreal—the subject matter, the treatment, everything. This is the way I see Redmond."

The mural at Nowhere High was a 1930s fantasy of cookie cutter kids tripping happily through a sunny, empty vacuum of a world. As far as T.J. could see, Josh's mural didn't tell any kind of linear story; it didn't come to neat conclusions. It had mill workers and street kids; the Jenner mansion was there, but so were the abandoned factories and the trailer park in the badlands. The faces weren't all white, and they weren't all smiling. And while there was sunlight on the painted river, in at least half the mural it was raining. T.J. grinned. That was the part of the mural he liked best; one thing he'd discovered it sure did a lot in Redmond, Pennsylvania was rain.

Alison and Josh joined the circle, curling up on the bean bag chair. T.J. poured himself some more eggnog. When he sat back, Caroline rested her head on his shoulder, and not for the first time, she read his mind. "Who do you think'll move into this place after we're gone?"

"We could give it back to Woofer," said Alison.

T.J. scanned the station thoughtfully—the mural, the posters, the Superman Christmas tree. "Or just leave it for whoever comes along and needs it. Those punks with the snowballs. The outsiders."

"It'll always be ours, though," Caro said. "I think we'll leave ghosts."

T.J. looked from the poster eyes of James Dean to the gold-green eyes of Caroline Buchanan. He knew what she meant. Six people's ghosts; the ghosts of love, friendship, laughter, loneliness, anger, strife, hope.

Yeah, T.J. thought, bending to kiss Caro. They'd leave part of themselves behind. But they'd take something with them, too.

If you need someone to talk to . . .

The kids in this book are lucky—when things get rough they can turn to each other. But if you have a problem and there isn't anyone you can talk to, here are some numbers you can call. They're toll free, and someone will be there to help twenty-four hours a day.

Covenant House: 1-800-999-9999
Drug and Alcohol Abuse Hotline:
    1-800-553-7160
Hit Home Runaway Hotline: 1-800-448-4663
National Child Abuse Hotline: 1-800-422-4453
National Institute on Drug Abuse:
    1-800-621-4000
National Runaway Hotline: 1-800-231-6946
National Runaway Switchboard and Suicide
    Hotline: 1-800-621-4000
Public Service AIDS Hotline: 1-800-447-AIDS
Runaway Hotline: 1-800-231-6946

If a family member abuses alcohol or you have a problem with cocaine, these numbers can direct you to help in your local area:

Alateen: 1-800-356-9996
1-800-COCAINE or 1-800-262-2463